Quim
Monzó

GASOLINE

Translated from the Catalan
by Mary Ann Newman

OPEN LETTER
LITERARY TRANSLATIONS FROM THE UNIVERSITY OF ROCHESTER

Library of Congress Cataloging-in-Publication Data:

Monzó, Quim, 1952-
    [Benzina. English]
    Gasoline / Quim Monzó ; translated from the Catalan by Mary Ann Newman.
      p. cm.
    ISBN-13: 978-1-934824-18-4 (pbk. : alk. paper)
    ISBN-10: 1-934824-18-6 (pbk. : alk. paper)
    I. Newman, Mary Ann. II. Title.
    PC3942.23.O53G37 2010
    849'.9354—dc22

                          2010004854

Translation of this novel was made possible thanks to the
support of the Ramon Llull Institut.

**LLLL institut
ramon llull**
Catalan Language and Culture

Printed on acid-free paper in the United States of America.

Text set in FF Scala, a serif typeface designed by Martin Majoor in 1990
for the Vredenburg Music Center in Utrecht, the Netherlands.

Design by N. J. Furl

Open Letter is the University of Rochester's nonprofit, literary translation press:
Lattimore Hall 411, Box 270082, Rochester, NY 14627

www.openletterbooks.org

For Mary Ann Newman

January

"Blow me down."
"I can't."
"In that case, let's go."
—Francesc Trabal, *L'any que ve*

O nce again, he feels as if he were asleep and awake at the same time, yet if he concentrates he feels as if he were fast asleep. A fraction of a second later, it dawns on him that perhaps Hildegarda is already awake, up and about, and (out of boredom) dressed, as he wastes time wondering whether or not he's awake. Then it all fades to gusts of wind, oranges, bicycles, a tin clown, a man jumping off a skyscraper, a tunnel, and a locomotive leaving a trail of smoke that, upon clearing, takes the shape of a street corner, a cafeteria with people inside. The dream is an exact reproduction of the scene in *Nighthawks* by Edward Hopper. He is thrilled to be able not only to identify the origin of the images in mid-dream, but also to be aware of doing it, and to remember that he had seen the painting as a little boy, many years before (impossible to calculate how many) at the Art Institute of Chicago. He also realizes that the painting is now appearing in this fantasy because the night before he had seen a reproduction of it in the window of a frame shop, along with two other reproductions of Hopper paintings. He remembers one of them: an office, and a secretary with a prominent ass (wearing a blue dress and glasses, he seems to recall) who is poring over a file cabinet, and a moth-eaten clerk sitting at his desk.

The diner, on the corner of two dark and deserted streets, has picture windows, a sign that reads PHILLIES, and a thin old waiter behind the counter, wearing a white soda jerk's hat. One woman and two men with wide-brimmed hats are sitting at the bar, drinking, but this doesn't last long because soon the diner is filling up with people: men identical (in face, hat, and suit) to the man or men already sitting there; and women identical (in face, hairdo, and dress) to the woman already at the counter (but wearing hats, fur stoles draped around their necks, and shiny handbags). Outside, in the street, there is a good layer of snow on the ground, and this is perfectly logical, because it's New Year's Eve, though in the painting he had seen as a child (and obviously in the reproduction he has seen the night before) there wasn't a trace of snow.

All at once, the people leave the bar and spill out onto the street, laughing. They leave by the dozens, by the hundreds. There are thousands of them, fleeing like insects. No matter how many leave, though, the diner is always full of people having vanilla, strawberry, raspberry, or chocolate milkshakes and crushed ice with a good squirt of blueberry, lemon, or mint syrup. It's just like that old movie gag in which (by circling out beyond the camera's range and circling back in again through an off-screen door) an endless stream of people gets out of a tiny car that could barely have seated four.

Of all the crowd, aside from the waiter, two characters always stay behind: the redhead dressed in burgundy and the man eating vanilla ice cream with chocolate syrup drizzled over it—who is he, himself (and he finds it hard to believe he hadn't recognized himself till now)—staring intently at the street where a car flashes by. Bit by bit the sky turns from black to dark blue, lights come on in a few windows; they go out when day breaks definitively, morning arrives implacably, and the diner ceases to be the silvery island it was during the night. The waiter sets up the counter with cups, teaspoons, knives, bread, jam, and butter. Not missing a beat, a stream of hungry office workers hurries into place, pushing and shoving, gulping down watery coffee, milk, toast, and croissants. As he has shifted his attention to the inside of the bar, the outside starts to go dark on him again. This is why, when he tries to light up the street again (at that point in mid-morning when all the office workers have left and the lonely people in the place are the man and the woman, or the woman and the two men, one of whom is he), the surroundings fade: everything goes white, stunningly resplendent, and turns into a beach. Oh, what a delightful sight, Hopper's diner smack in the middle of a beach with plastic chairs and a string of desolate awnings, and, in the distance, a backdrop of immobile waves spotted with surfing teenagers. Finally he feels he's dreaming freely: he resolves to let his imagination flow. The woman in the burgundy dress is wearing sunglasses, as is the waiter. The other man is and isn't there, appearing and disappearing. When he takes off his hat (and the shadow that hides his face vanishes), Heribert recognizes himself unmistakably, sweating beyond endurance in his steaming woolen winter coat.

The dream has been boring him for some time now. He tries to stop it, but he can't. Now he sees them in bathing suits: himself in shiny black briefs and her in one of those backless skintight suits with two strips of cloth stretching up from the waist in front, covering the breasts and tying around the neck. They are rolling down a flight of stairs and he crashes into a glass door that softly gives. For a fraction of a second, Heribert (about to dive into the water) asks himself if the woman isn't Helena. Now they are swimming, off on their own, surviving the gigantic waves that engulf them. They swim in silence, and when Heribert plunges deeper, he wishes he didn't ever have to surface again. He seems to stay underwater for hours. When he does surface, she is already on the beach, walking slowly towards the diner. He rushes after her. When he reaches the sand, he steps on a small black cockroach. Hildegarda's voice (was it Hildegarda, then, and not Helena?) tells him to hurry, to go faster, because she has to leave. Now he's running, trying not to step on any of the thousands of roaches streaming out from under the sand. When he looks up, he tries to sight the cafeteria, but it is nowhere to be found: the beach is a long sliver, absolute and deserted, on which two figures are running: the woman and the other man who is finally there, and he seems to have seized the opportunity to run off with her (which proves that the whole game of appearing and disappearing was just a ruse to seem inconspicuous and then be free to make off with the woman). He thinks: if only I could remember the man's face . . . ; if only I had seen his face . . . ; if only I could start dreaming another dream . . . He has a premonition that he will never dream again, and he flees through passageways between buildings, silent basements, swimming rough waves beating against the ships, going back to a port, to a city square at night, to the diner on the old street, with the woman dressed in burgundy and a man in a dark suit whose hat brim hides his face, wondering whether the figure of a second man will emerge, a shriek, a blow to the chin, the earth splitting open as he laughs, the fall.

•

A sharp noise awakens him. First he thinks maybe the bottle of champagne has fallen on the floor and shattered, but he slides his foot along until he finds the bottle right where he remembered leaving it: by the side of the bed. Then he figures it must be the shade banging against the windowpanes. Then he opens his eyes and shifts around under the sheets. Maybe it was a cat on the roof, or one of the wicker chairs on the balcony blown over by the wind, or maybe the glass ball has struck the banister. He sits up and touches his head. It hurts. He remembers the window shade again: it must have crashed into the glass, harder than ever before. Or maybe it had been a thief with a mask and a striped jersey who slipped in through the dining room window? Or a hit man with a long, black, shiny getaway car waiting out in front, with the motor running, who has jimmied the door open and is now coming slowly up the stairs, feeling his way along to that very room where he would now kill him? Or maybe it's Helena herself (Helena would certainly have no need to hire a hit man) who suddenly feels like . . . ?

He yawns. Yawning makes you sleepy. He closes his eyes tighter. He tries to go back to sleep.

He can't. He lifts his head. He runs a finger along Hildegarda's shoulder. He kisses her ear. In the half-light he looks at her back, her hips . . . He squeezes his eyelids shut. He tries to pick up the thread of the dream again, but it eludes him; the more he tries to remember it, the faster it flees. He only remembers the beach . . . If it were summer, he'd get up and run out to the ocean for a swim. Some people have a tradition of swimming on a certain day in the winter. In Barcelona they swim across the port. On New Year's Day? The Feast of the Kings? Christmas? He remembers the beach full of spots, like red caviar. All at once, he can make out the counter, the waiter, the woman.

He saw the painting for the first time when he was thirteen, as a father in well-pressed trousers dragged him from one gallery of the museum to the next (until the moment he discovered the painting, after which the hard part was dragging him away from it). *Nighthawks* had mesmerized him. Many years later, when a critic averred (in passing in some article) that Hopper was a precursor of the hyperrealists, Heribert read it with surprise. It was a devaluation and, to some extent, an injustice to categorize him (and thus to label, limit, judge him, and store him in formaldehyde) as a mere precursor of the hyperrealists, when in any Hopper there was much more (a web of memory, of desire) than in all that evaporated outpouring of canvases filled with ketchup, French fries, and shiny cars. He knows full well why he dreamed of it. Because the night before, in the shop window, he looked at it coldly and thought it really wasn't such a big deal after all, and maybe if he were to come across it now for the first time he wouldn't find it so exceptional. He yawns again; he decides to shut his eyes, but they are already shut.

There is no getting around it. He squeezes his eyes even tighter and thinks of the girl he saw last night at the party (wearing a magician's hat covered with cardboard stars and a silvery moon) who was eating the twelve grapes of New Year's by the handful and choking. He retrieves the image. He stands next to her. He smiles. The girl smiles back. They quickly down their drinks (Hildegarda is off in a corner of the room, dancing alone) and, hand in hand, they go outside. They sit on a stoop behind some bushes; he strokes her thighs, she strokes his chest.

He is tired of fantasizing, but he persists. The girl, naked . . . ; no, not naked: wearing a skirt but no underwear. No, wearing black panties but no bra; no: white panties . . . He feels like sleeping, but he's not sleepy.

He checks the time: four o'clock. Only a little over an hour ago, he got into bed swearing that next New Year's Eve he'd go to sleep at 9:00 p.m. He licks Hildegarda's back and waist and she shivers and shifts in her sleep.

He turns on the light on the night table. He picks up a book lying there. *A coleira do cão.* He starts to read.

He reads eighty pages. Then he stops. It's not that he's bored; he's just not in the mood any more. He gets up, puts on his pants, lifts the shade a crack, flips the switch to the outside light, looks out at the snow-covered balcony, and the beach, farther on, black as the sky. He opens the door to the balcony: an icy gust of wind and the sound of the waves come in. He closes it at once.

In the kitchen he makes coffee and adds a splash of milk. He opens the shades. If a vampire were to appear now at the window and look at him, fangs at the ready, he would consider it the most predictable thing in the world.

He raises the shades in the living room, the dining room, in all the rooms. With the cup of coffee in his hand, he sits on the throw rug next to the bed where Hildegarda is still sleeping. He lets his eyes wander around the room and stops at the window. A round spot is reflected in the glass: the lamp on the night table. He looks at the window frame, the shutters, and the strips between the panes of glass . . . "What do you call the slats between the windowpanes? There has to be a specific name for them. Every object has a specific name." He looks at the windowsill and thinks: "Now that's a windowsill. But what are the lateral 'sills' called? And the opposite of the windowsill, the upper 'sill'? What about the edge of the windowsill, does that have a name? Does the name change according to whether the edge is squared or rounded?" He goes down to the living room, searches among the books, finds a dictionary; he takes it out, goes upstairs, and sits down by the bed again. He opens it at random and reads: board (bōrd, bôrd), n., 1. Daily meals, esp. as provided for pay: *Ten dollars a day for room and board.* —v.t., 2. To furnish with meals, or with meals and lodging, esp. for pay: *They boarded him for $20 a week.* —v.i., 3. to take one's meals, or be supplied with food and lodging at a fixed price: *Several of us boarded at the same rooming house.* He shuts the book. He opens it again: georgic (jor´jik), adj., 1. agricultural. —n., 2. a poem on an agricultural theme. Syn. 1, 2. bucolic. *Georgics, The,* a didactic poem (39-29 B.C.) by Virgil.

He goes on reading at random. A few hours later, he closes the book and leaves it on the floor, and he sits watching as, bit by bit, the sun appears beyond the horizon and the first dawn of the year sheds an imperceptible light on all things below: the water, the sand on the beach, the folded umbrellas, the chairs on the balcony, the slats on the windows, the windowsill, the floor where he is sitting, the furniture, his own feet, which he stares at for quite a while as if they were two monsters. Then he hears Hildegarda waking up, and he sits on the bed, feeling her gaze on the nape of his neck. He doesn't turn around until she traces the length of his spine with her fingernail.

·

Afterwards, he is completely overcome with sleep. When he opens his eyes again, the sun (a pale, faint sun) is high in the sky and Hildegarda is sitting in the armchair with a blue robe on (sky blue, bluer by far than today's gray sky), painting her toenails, each nail a different color: one pink, one blue, one gold, one black, one purple, one white, one silver, one yellow, and one gray.

Hildegarda is reconstructing the (approximately) two weeks they've been involved, weighing the pros and cons of their relationship. Heribert thinks that the terms she's using ("involved," "our relationship") are mere euphemisms. Euphemisms for what, though? What does "involved" mean? The two weeks we've spent touching each other? "Touching each other" sounds like another euphemism to him, though. "The two weeks we've spent kissing and caressing each other's genitals?" He finds the last expression cold enough to be accurate. Then he turns his attention entirely to what Hildegarda is saying to him: everything he hears is a euphemism.

"You don't know," she's saying, "how hard it was for me to convince Tiziana I wasn't coming here. She wanted to come along. 'You go there every year and you never invite me,' she said. She said that I always say I'm not coming and then I always come. That's why I'm afraid she might surprise us and show up with a bouquet of flowers and a box of chocolates. She gets more and more melancholy every year, and she wants someone to put up with her gloom, and, frankly, I just can't do it any more. Not only that, why should I be the one to get stuck holding her hand when Marino's gone. She should call him. I can't stand her dependency. And not only that, but I wouldn't like her to know that you and I . . . can you imagine? You didn't like Tiziana at all, did you? But the party was a lot of fun. Didn't you think so? Marino didn't like her much at the beginning, either, and now look at them . . . Everyone changes. Even him. He's a strange guy. Not because he changes. He's strange for lots of reasons; he goes off on these tangents. You artists are all a little strange, no matter what field you're in, or at least you all pretend to be. And not just artists, either. I used to get along so well with him. Now it's as if he weren't interested in me at all. I used to study (have I told you this?) in a school of *bel canto*. I wanted to sing in the opera. Have you ever sung, opera or anything? Or done anything onstage, like acting? I really love the feeling of being onstage . . . I know what it's like, because I've been there, in the chorus, and I know the feeling of being alone before the abyss of the audience. ('The abyss of the audience . . .' that's pretty good, isn't it?) I've never been up there alone, of course, but I know what I'm saying. You feel alone all the same, no matter how many people are up there with you. Tiziana used to sing with me. We met at the school. I met Marino in my last year, before I sang in the chorus. He was the one who got me into the chorus, because he was really pursuing me back then. Not any more. He's such a great singer, and he always has so much work that he doesn't have any time for me. I don't know what I stopped liking first: him or the opera. I've come to realize that opera is not what I thought it was, what I dreamed of. Do you think I've become disillusioned because I married an opera singer? (Perhaps I shouldn't just say *a* singer, but the *best* singer, but I don't want to brag; though it isn't really bragging if I'm not talking about myself, is it?) There was a time when I wanted to write. (I've already told you that, haven't I?) I was a teenager . . . The other day I heard a piece I really loved. No, it was jazz. Now I'm starting to like jazz. It was called *Blue Rondo à la Turk*, and it's by the Dave Brubeck Quartet. You've heard it? Oh, since I don't know much about jazz yet, I didn't realize it was very well known . . . You have the record? With *Take Five*? What's *Take Five*? Oh. Would you lend it to me? Oh, I'm so thrilled. Please lend it to me. Don't forget. Maybe some day . . . No, forget it. No . . . well, maybe some day . . . I'd like to try jazz. But I don't know which instrument would be best for me. No, no, it's out of the question. Painting is the thing that totally absorbs me now, ever since I married Marino and abandoned opera. I think I should try having a show. Contact with the public is essential, isn't it? How can a body of work evolve if it doesn't come into contact with the viewers it's meant for? I'm not hinting around, but we've known each other for a while now . . . No, I don't want to show you my paintings, it's too embarrassing. Anyway, I don't know if I'm still interested in painting. But I've been saying I'm not interested any more for a couple of years now, and I'm still at it. No, no. I'd be too embarrassed, you're too good. Give me a kiss. Mmm. All right, if you promise not to make fun of me, I'll show them to you. Really. We can arrange it some other time. But you have to be very honest. If you don't like them, say so. I don't want you humoring me. I couldn't bear it! Are you in a hurry? I'll drive you into the city. I have to go home, too; I have so much to do . . . I've had a wonderful time, though, all these days we've spent together. It was nice to start the year with you. Do you think it's a good sign? For you or for me? Don't you have anything to say? Give me a great big hug. We'll get together soon, won't we? I'll let you off at the subway stop, okay?"

I n the subway, sitting between a woman thin as a bag of bones and a man sleeping with his head between his knees, Heribert thinks that usually by this time of day he would already have been at work in the studio for three hours. Then he finds it strange to have thought "usually," since lately he is there less and less, and he finds it easier and easier to come up with excuses, again "usually," not to be there.

Across from him, a man is moving in syncopated time: he is drumming on the ground with his feet, as if following the rhythm of a song, but he isn't wearing earphones and there is no radio on. At the next stop, this man and the man sleeping with his head between his knees get off with Heribert. The man moving in syncopated time stays on the platform, waiting for the express, and Heribert goes out into the street.

He walks into the bookstore and, as he goes through the turnstile, realizes that at no point had he been aware where his steps were leading him. Going in there was always dangerous; an afternoon might go up in smoke, as it could very well be (and, in fact, always is) several hours before he goes out again. That bookstore, divided into two enormous spaces on either side of the street, with two big splendid floors in each of the spaces, draws him like a circus show. He has always found libraries and bookstores more seductive than the books themselves. He likes to look at the rows of bindings. He likes to run his hands over the covers of the encyclopedias and dictionaries, open a volume at random to see the illustrations, stroke the glossy coated paper, peer closely at the letters till they reveal their hairy edges, their distortions. Ever since he decided, two months before, never to attend another art exhibit (they were all so mediocre), he sees everything around him as if it were an art exhibit and discovers unsuspected facets to every object.

The children's books were on the ground floor. Children's books bother him. It bothers him precisely that they are *for children*. He has never understood by what rights someone decides there is a dividing line that makes some books *for children*, some *for adults*, others *erotic*, still others *porno*, and, finally, those even farther beyond, *romance*. And it also bothers him that a whole line of shelves should display the title *poetry*. What do they mean by "poetry"? Or "romance"?

As soon as he sets foot on the escalator, he turns around so as to go up backwards and watch as the ground floor gets farther and farther away: the entrance, the turnstiles, the cash registers, the two immense tables of bargain books. When he realizes he has thought *bargain* books, his stomach turns. Isn't that definition just as presumptuous as one that attributes amorous, poetic, or mysterious qualities to books while—nevertheless—he finds the former to be quite reasonable? At least until now. He feels like a child, playing at discovering already discovered things. When he turns around to get off the escalator and step onto terra firma, however, he realizes (as one enlightened, not knowing why) that the really childish thing is to refuse to admit that it is good for things to be classified; despite the imperfections of the labels, this is the only way to delimit them, understand them, control them, grasp them. (And to have designated that thought as *childish* is equally childish: no doubt about it; and the fact that he has to resort to another adjective in order to dismiss the first series of adjectives as stupid confirms it.) When he reaches the top, and lets his eyes wander over the signs in the different sections (cooking, home improvement, pocket books, textbooks, mysteries, art, fiction, new releases, bestsellers . . .), he feels that the most logical thing in the world is precisely for them to be classified. If not, what chaos! Even the sign that says *poetry* seems coherent and logical. Everyone knows what is to be found under that caption, and it is precisely that which makes it not merely valid, but indispensable. He even understands that the books on the shelves labeled *mystery* must, of necessity, be far from the shelves of the *bestsellers*. And if the book is both a *mystery* and a *bestseller*, it must be found under *bestsellers*, as this is the characteristic (additional, and thus more evident) that distinguishes it quite beyond its intrinsic mysteriousness. Always and ever, the surface of things: the part that can be touched and seen without need of opening and destroying it to find out what its innards are like. How is it possible that until now he has not perceived the wisdom of these classifications? It is evident, moreover, that the books in the *fiction* department must of necessity be there, and by no means in *literature*. He feels as if a long time has elapsed since those classifications so annoyed him with their arbitrariness, and yet it isn't so: he was still laboring under that absurd misconception when he stepped on the escalator. (But he isn't entirely wrong: for three weeks now—or perhaps a month—he has not been so sure of things as he used to be; it seems as if he has been changing imperceptibly and is no longer the same person: it could be, then, that what he was thinking as he stepped on the escalator was simply a thought born of his former self-assurance, and what has happened as he rose on the escalator is that, imperceptibly, he has begun to realize that the thought no longer jibes with his present state.) Once, in the beforehand that is becoming—more and more, and without his knowing why—irremediably distant, he had tried to figure out the systems and expose the contradictions hidden among the bookcases: Steinbeck was under *fiction*, and Hardy under *literature*. In those days he had found it arbitrary and had deduced that they considered literature to have died in the nineteenth century and, from that moment on, everything was *fiction*. But there were also flaws in that line of reasoning: Kafka was under *literature*. What was he doing there? He had reasoned that perhaps those twentieth-century authors whose lives had a certain, let's say, tragic quality were sent to swell the shelves of literature. But now it is all clear to him: it's *obvious* that Hardy and Kafka are *literature*, and Steinbeck, *fiction*. Why rock the boat? Even more to the point: in order for things to be useful to us, they must not be resisted, but accepted just as they are. He feels a chill at the nape of his neck. He pulls up the lapels of his coat but then realizes he's hot: the heat is on so high that he's sweating. He takes off his coat.

He peruses the art books. He leafs through one on Tamara de Lempicka, one on Hopper (which brings back snatches of the dream . . .), one on Matisse (that shows red flowers with violet spots that seem to move), and one on Magritte. Were there cockroaches there, too? He looks at the legs of the tables where the books lie, expecting to find termites. There aren't any. He goes back to the book, turns the page, and sees the drawing of a pipe bearing the legend *Ceci n'est pas une pipe*. "It most certainly is not," he thinks, feeling vaguely content.

He puts down the book on Magritte and picks up a few more books at random from another table, without looking at the titles. He sits in an armchair in a corner of the room. He watches the people who walk by. From time to time he leafs through one of the books, then another, pleased at being capable—despite his leafing-through—of not knowing what they are about. It is the books he's interested in, not what they say. What they say awakens no passion at all. (Amazing to have felt this way for so long, only to be reasoning it through now for the first time!) Perhaps reasoning it through is a step backwards, though, because, in fact, feelings lie more on the surface of things. It is easy from him not to know what the books say. It is just a question of not noticing, of making an effort not to notice. It's strange what's happening to him: attitudes he would previously have considered stupid now delight him, and he finds honest and worthy those which at any previous moment he would have considered idiotic. Maybe he is evolving, becoming more mature. In an on-the-spot application of the ideas fluttering in his head, he sees that leafing through those books comes down, in the end, to a series of arbitrary gestures; and he finds it quite fine to be making arbitrary gestures. Why is it quite fine to be making arbitrary gestures? He doesn't feel like responding and even considers it stupid to have posed the question. He finds thinking to be a bore. He finds this boredom to be another symptom of maturity. He lets his eyes wander over the shelves, trying not to register anything. He sees a girl leafing through a book and looking from side to side. He realizes right away that she wants to steal it. The girl looks behind her and meets Heribert's gaze. The sudden flash of her eyes confirms Heribert's impression that she wanted to steal the book that now, quite flustered, she is quickly returning to the shelf. In spite of his irritation at having realized what the girl had in mind (and therefore at not being able to continue running his eyes over things without registering them), he considers getting up, approaching her, and telling her to take the book without a second thought, as she's mistaken if she's taken him for a guard, or if she has taken his expression of curiosity for one of reproach.

When Heribert gets up, the girl has already disappeared behind some bookcases. He searches all over the room for her and only discovers her when, from the handrail, he casts an eye over the main floor: she is at the cash register, paying, waiting for the cashier to put a paperback in a bag, and darting quick glances at the escalator.

Heribert finds it illogical to leave without a book. It isn't exactly illogical: it is somehow suspect. Suspect? In what way? The question also seems stupid to him. To punish himself, as he runs toward the table of art books and picks up a copy of the one on Tamara de Lempicka, he pinches his left arm with the fingers of his right hand. He is still running (and feeling upon his skin the stares of all the salespeople and customers), when he goes down the escalator. For a moment it seems strange that no one thinks he has stolen anything, but by the following moment it seems evident that no one who had stolen anything would run; so it wasn't even necessary for him to buy a book: breaking into a sprint was quite enough. As he puts on his coat after paying at one of the cash registers, he sees the girl far away, across the street, walking south.

He crosses the avenue (so suddenly that two taxis collide in order not to hit him) and follows her, quickening his pace until he's close enough not to lose sight of her. Then he slows up. He is all set to approach her and say: "I'm terribly sorry. I'm not a guard at that bookstore. I know you decided not to steal the book on my account: when I looked at you, you must have thought it was a reproach, but it wasn't at all."

He watches her walking in front of him. He thinks she looks like an Anna and doesn't feel like trying to figure out why he thinks her name should be Anna and not Judith or Cynthia. Maybe Anne or Ann, or perhaps Carmen or Barbara; not Mary, though. He doesn't know why, but he's sure a girl who walks like that can't be a Mary.

He falls into step with her and walks right by her side. After a while, though, he reflects that he can't address her without conveying an intention quite extraneous to the pure and simple message he wishes to deliver. From close up, her face seems familiar, and from more than one occasion. He sees it against a backdrop of paintings or sculptures . . . At some exhibit? He starts to feel embarrassed, or shy, or scared, and he keeps looking at her, determined to say nothing even before her glance (surprised, both angry and frightened), makes him decide to diminish his speed, just as she accelerates. "Lately, I just seem to ruin everything," he thinks. And, right after that, "It would have been more compelling to think 'Lately, I just seem to ruin everything' with tears in my eyes."

·

He takes a quick look in all the rooms. As usual, Helena isn't there. He thinks of preparing lunch, but at that point in the afternoon he decides it is more appropriate to skip lunch and prepare dinner. What, though? He opens the refrigerator and checks off the contents: ice cubes, a bottle of vodka, two bottles of white wine, butter, shrimp, chicken, beef, jams, several kinds of bread, tomatoes, string beans, corn, orange soda, grape-fruit juice, tomato juice, sparkling water, onions, potatoes, olives, capers. The mere thought of figuring out what he could do with all that makes him dizzy. Perhaps only to avoid any more such musings, he decides that, precisely because it is so late, he can take advantage of these last moments of daylight: he goes up to his studio, prepares his paints, and turns on the radio. Without much enthusiasm, he continues filling in small strips of black on a canvas with a charcoal sketch of a man sitting on a stool with his head propped up on a bar.

Since this gets boring, he picks up the book he bought. He examines it, he touches it. He is so sure he'll like it (both the book and every one of the plates, including the ones he's never seen) that he puts off opening it. The longer he delays in opening the front cover and looking at the first page, the longer he puts off the pleasure of beginning to read it, the longer he will postpone the end. He also realizes that the sooner he begins to read it, the sooner he will finish it. (He quickly sees that this is just the same thing said backwards. For a moment he is surprised that one can say the same thing by saying it backwards. He perceives immediately that this is painfully obvi-ous. Being surprised at self-evident things makes him feel corroded.)

For a while, he halfheartedly mulls over the thought that everything goes by (or everything has gone by him) too quickly in life. Then he won-ders whether he isn't putting off starting the book because, in fact, he's not in the mood. Or is it this long line of thought he's not in the mood for? More than a long line: an interminable line. He goes down to the living room. He turns on the television, goes to the kitchen, opens the refrigerator, takes out the bottle of vodka, pours himself a glass, goes back to the living room, sits down on the couch, and starts watching television. He remembers, though, that he hasn't cleaned his brushes or turned off the radio. So he gets up, leaves the glass on the end table (and as he does it thinks that he ought to leave it on a coaster). Then it crosses his mind that he promised Hildegarda he would take her the record of the Dave Brubeck Quartet the next time they got together. He starts looking for it so he will know where it is when the time comes. One by one, he checks all the record covers, from the first to the last. Since he doesn't come across it, he checks them all again, from the last to the first. When he's done, he remembers that a few weeks ago Helena had lent it to Hipòlita. He sits down again in front of the television set just as a movie comes on. He is pleased to have arrived just in time.

Quite some time later, he realizes he doesn't know what's happening onscreen. He has seen the picture from the beginning, but now he wouldn't be capable of explaining the plot. He decides to try: on the screen, two heterosexual couples (Heterosexual? he asks himself. Maybe it would be better to say of different sexes.) are arguing about he's not sure what at a table in a restaurant. He uses the remote control to distort the colors: the people's skin turns a reddish pink, like plastic, and the green of the tablecloth is practically fluorescent. It all seems so unreal, with that nervous drizzle that the color casts on actors and objects alike that, in the end, he feels better about it and is able to continue looking at the film without concerning himself with the plot or the actors' gestures.

Two hours later his own snoring awakens him. He turns off the television and drags himself to bed.

·

He hears the rustling of sheets and asks himself if it is the rustling that has awakened him or if, a few moments before, he heard shoes hitting the floor, or if it's just that, since he heard the rustling of sheets, he thinks he ought to have heard the sound of Helena undressing. Even if she folded her clothes carefully, shoes (in the quiet of the night) usually make noise when they hit the wood floor, and it is this sound that always awakens him. But what about earlier? Had he heard the floorboards creak under Helena's feet? It worries him not to be able to tell exactly which sound has awakened him. It worries him that, little by little, he seems to be losing his previous auditory sensitivity; he used to have total awareness of the sounds around him, even when he was fast asleep, right down to the movements that had produced them.

His back feels cold. In a few minutes, Helena's body, which is cold at the moment, will be warm, and it will be nice to turn over and put his arms around her, as if in his sleep. He thinks the scene would make a beautiful painting: a double bed, with a man sleeping on one edge and on the other a woman lifting the covers to get in. How would you know, though, whether she was lifting them to get in or out? This thought makes the image dissolve, and since he is absolutely certain he will not be able to retrieve it, he doesn't even try. He continues to pretend to be sleeping, as if he weren't aware that Helena had arrived. He opens one eye, and since from that position he can see neither the numbers nor the luminescent hands of the alarm clock on the night table, he shifts, as if he were dreaming, and (with his back still to Helena) positions his head in such a way that, by opening one eye, he can see the time: 4:15. He wonders whether to turn over and embrace her or wait for her to do it. Why is it that lately she doesn't?

He hears her breathing regularly. Is it possible that she has already fallen asleep? All those endless meetings to set up the summer shows . . . He had always thought that even summer shows were programmed years (or at least many months) in advance. Helena, though, has such a nose for the new, such an ability to capture the pulse of the moment, that she can't plan her shows more than a few months ahead. He has a nice long yawn and tries to go back to sleep. The image of a cockroach appears to him and, as hard as he struggles to erase it, it persists, leaving him more and more wide awake. Then he hears Helena breathing deeply, fast asleep. Before dozing off again (or waking up, as for days now—and, above all, since the night before—it is as if he were sleeping awake or as if he were living asleep) he opens an eye one last time to look at the clock: it's 5:30.

.

Lately, he enjoys sleeping late more and more. Before, whenever he wasn't out carousing the previous night, Heribert would get up about 9:00 (neither too late nor too early, he would tell himself), shower, have citrus juice for breakfast, and, around 10:00 or 10:30, go up to the studio, turn on the radio or the record player (now it tended more and more to be the radio, since having to choose which records he wanted to hear put him off), and paint until 2:00. Then he would have lunch—at home if Helena was there, at a restaurant if she wasn't, since cooking for himself was a bore. The problem is that, tired of always going to the same restaurant, for some six months now he has been having lunch at a different place every day, and so, every time Helena isn't home for lunch, he has to go farther away since (even counting the times—not frequent—that he's cheated and gone twice to the same place) he has been to all the restaurants in the neighborhood and in the neighboring neighborhoods. Once or twice he has even taken the subway, crossed the river, and had lunch outside the city. But this isn't his usual pattern, since it prevents his returning in the afternoon to start painting again (particularly now that he was preparing a double show which, according to Hug and Helena was to be the definitive proof that his triumph of the previous year is irrevocable), and it is imperative that he work in the afternoon because things are not proceeding at their usual pace. This is why he has abandoned his old routine (or lack of one) of doing nothing in the afternoon. Before, on occasion, he would go home, read, or watch TV or a video; or sometimes he would go out and have a look at the art shows. Other times (but definitely only once in a while) he did none of those three things and instead would go to the movies. Now, in his haste to do the paintings for the show, he goes back home and shuts himself up in the studio, to paint or to plan possible paintings (except on weekends and holidays, unless for some reason he considers it imperative). These last weeks, even though he's been taking notes, at most he's finished a couple of paintings he considers mediocre; and the date on which they would have to begin hanging the paintings in the two galleries is approaching at a rate that increases daily.

In the evenings, he meets up with friends. Mostly with Hug and Hilari, for dinner. Afterwards their schedules are anything but predictable, and even though he tries not to get home too late, so he'll be able to get up early and get back to work, he still finds it equally hard to get up. Lately, what he likes best of all is to stay in bed and stare at the ceiling.

•

At nine o'clock sharp, the telephone rings. Helena stirs, buries her head in the pillow so as not to hear it, and goes on sleeping. Feeling his way, Heribert picks up the receiver. It's Hilari, proposing dinner that evening. Hilari will bring along some girls he knows. They make arrangements. He hangs up. Heribert feels the sleep in his eyes, like fists, but he is too wide awake to go back to sleep.

Ten minutes later he is sitting with a half-grapefruit in front of him, which he is eating, section by section, with the aid of a serrated spoon. When he's finished, he goes up to the studio, sits before the easel, prepares the paints, and continues painting black sections on the canvas of the man sitting on a stool. He is so tired that it is an effort for him to finish working on the man's suit and the wood of the bar. A half hour later he hears noise in the kitchen, assumes it's Helena who's gotten up, and goes downstairs. While she spreads blueberry jam on a piece of rye bread, he opens a bottle of white wine and pours himself a glass.

"You look sleepy," she says. "Give me a kiss. It's the first one this year, you know. Mmm . . . That's nice. First of all, Happy New Year, okay? How's it going for you? Mine's been just perfect. I had a great time. You know how much I like that city. It's small without being depressing. It's a shame you couldn't come. One New Year's Eve Hannah and I went to eat at a German restaurant, just gorgeous, where the waiters wore black vests and long white aprons all the way down to mid-calf. It was like being back at the turn of the century. And her house is just beautiful, a half hour outside the city. Did you get a lot or work done? You must be just about finished. I'll be up in a few minutes to see what you've done. No? You've got to get a move on, sweetheart; there are only three weeks left. And at this rate . . . Did I say three? In two weeks they've got to be setting it all up. I'm tired of always running ragged at the last minute. At least you (you of all people) could have a little consideration for me. You're not going to throw all this work out the window, now, are you? You wouldn't be the first. This past year things have been going so well for you . . . With Hug you were getting along, but when you and I got together, it was perfection! This isn't about me, it's about the gallery, and (heck, why not?) about me, too. If you would only listen to me and . . . Why do you keep Hug on? Are you going to carry him all your life? Could Hug ever have gotten you the press I've gotten you since February? You don't give me enough credit. You don't listen to me.

You listen to him, though. I'm going to call him and have him give you a talking-to. He should at least be good for that. I really think you trust him more than you trust me. Sure he got the world press to lie down at your feet, but I had already broken the ground for you. Who got the city papers to bow down to you? To get other countries to recognize you afterwards was easy. But here, it certainly wasn't easy. And why did I do it? Because I love you. Come on, give me a kiss. Do you like my hair? You haven't said a word about it. Now I ought to make a scene, like in the comics, when the husband comes home and doesn't notice that his wife has a new hairdo. I had it done at Hannah's hairdressers. And then I was so busy, I couldn't even call you. Well, not that night, of course; that night we had people over for drinks to celebrate the summer program. In the summer a lot of novices come through and put even more thought into the organization so we don't fill the summer shows with leftovers. What time is it? Getting up late makes the day so short. I've got to run. Mmmm . . . I've got a date with Hipòlita. Button me up, please. Thanks. Give me a little kiss. I won't be home for lunch. And get a move on!"

S ince neither of them feels like going to a restaurant, as soon as Hug arrives Heribert begins to prepare the shrimp. Now, sitting face to face, across a table set with a white tablecloth, Heribert and Hug are devouring them. As he peels one, Heribert thinks that the shell of a shrimp isn't all that different from the shell of a cockroach. He opens another bottle of white wine.

"Kid," says Hug, "I'm here to give you a good talking-to, but since you're certainly old enough to know what you're doing, I'll just remind you that we could lose our shirts here. No temper tantrums, now, and no weird, outlandish games. All artists have creative crises (if that's what you want to call them, even though I think it's ridiculous), and all artists get over them, and even if they don't, they pretend they do and keep on going. Maybe what you need is to have a little fun. Go out with some girls. You certainly don't have to worry about Helena at this stage of the game, right? You don't get out to clear the cobwebs enough. Not only that, you let all kinds of opportunities pass you by, and, believe me, you do have opportunities . . . You weren't like this before; you were more lighthearted. Until a few months ago, you were always telling me about one affair or another. You've been slowing down, going out less and less. Or are you going out and just not telling me? I'd never forgive you for holding out on me. I'd be incredibly pissed at your lack of faith. And if I say you let opportunities pass you by, it's because Hildegarda—whom you, of all people introduced me to—is a babe, and if you were interested . . . Well, she's really into you. I'm sure of it, because five or six days ago we arranged to get together for a moment because she had been calling me ever since you introduced us, to show me her work, but since I thought it was odd, the way she looks at you,

that you weren't already involved, I kept putting her off, saying I was busy
. . . Did you know she used to sing in the opera? She even sang at the Met.
Did you already know that, or are you just not surprised? In the chorus,
but she sang there, and not everyone gets that far, not even in the chorus.
Stop laughing. Now it seems she's decided to paint, and so she finally got
me up to her house to show me her work. Her husband is in Europe, on a
tour, since he's an opera singer, and, listen, you can't imagine how good it
was. It's been years since I met a woman who melted like butter at the first
touch. With such soft, full lips . . . and those enormous eyes. I'm telling
you this, so you'll stop being a fool and go for it. And then, get down to
work, because in two (two or three?), well, in two or three weeks we have
to start hanging canvases. Call her. Really. I don't mind. You know how we
used to . . . remember the trouble we used to get into? Boy."

Heribert is surprised not to be amazed. Then he is surprised at being
surprised. Why should he have been amazed? What about Hildegarda,
wouldn't she figure out that he and Hug knew each other, and that it was
more than likely they would talk about their affairs? He imagines this
must be what she wants. Hug lifts his empty glass, and Heribert rushes
to open a third bottle of white wine.

When Helena arrives they are eating chocolate cookies and drinking
coffee and cognac. She's arrived in a sweat, carrying two bags from a
department store. She kisses each of them on the cheek. Hug helps her
put one of the bags on the table, and quickly says goodbye and leaves.

Heribert goes up to the studio. He finds the morning's colors all pre-
pared, a little dry. He sits down. He stares at the painting. He dips the
brush into the paint mechanically. The boredom that engulfs him is so
great he messes up the application of the paint to the legs of the stool.
If he keeps on painting, he'll ruin it altogether. "If I can't overcome this
boredom," he thinks, "I won't be able to go on." He continues painting and
ruins the canvas beyond repair. "At least I've been . . ." He doesn't know
whether to finish the thought with the word *sincere*, or *honest*, or *consistent*.
He hears Helena turn on the television. He goes on working despite the
fact that each brushstroke wreaks new havoc on the painting.

A half hour later, he considers the painting to be an absolute disaster.
He takes it off the easel, half resting it, half throwing it against the wall.
He hears Helena turn off the television and tell him she's leaving, she has

to go to the gallery to see if they've picked up some lithographs, and if they haven't, to make sure they do so immediately. As he hears the door close, Heribert places a new, bigger, canvas on another easel.

·

An hour later, he looks at the new painting, screws up his face into an expression of disgust, takes it off the easel, and throws it on top of the first one. He quickly cleans the brushes and paint and, in doing so, stains his pants. He wonders whether to shower and finally opts for the most passive route: not showering. He changes his pants, doesn't change his t-shirt, puts a jacket on over it, then a coat and boots. He goes out into the street and into the subway. On the platform he decides to get off at the sixth stop. "Because six is an insignificant number, a petty number. It's not brilliant like three, or pleasant like two, or magical like seven, or independent like one, or . . ." He boards the train. He closes his eyes. So he won't see the next station and therefore won't know which line he's on (which would have made it impossible for him not to figure out what the sixth stop would be), he mentally hums an obsessive tune.

On the street, he buys three papers at the first newsstand he comes across. He walks down the avenue, never stepping on snow that has already been stepped on. This reminds him of when, as a child in Barcelona, he would walk down the street trying to step only on alternating paving stones, on the diagonal, like in a game of checkers, feeling that, if he missed, a tremendous curse would fall upon him. Every so often, he makes clouds with his breath. He sees a bar with a long window-front. It's one of those bars he's always disliked: too clean, quiet, unnecessarily expensive, and with an annoying tendency to be frequented by people favoring hot chocolate and lattes. He goes in and sits down. It's hot. He takes off his coat and jacket. He picks up one of the newspapers, looks at the front page, and sees that none of the headlines interests him in the least. He looks over the room: it's almost empty. There is just one couple, across the room, sitting very close and having espresso. From behind the bar a waiter is approaching, notebook in hand. Heribert understands his purpose. He feels terrified. He doesn't know what to order.

"What should I have?"

The waiter's expression shows that he thinks he's either an obnoxious character who's trying to give him a hard time or a snob who likes to be waited on down to the smallest detail. Nevertheless, with a smile on his face, he recites:

"A beer? An espresso? A scotch? A bourbon? Pernod? Fernet? Rum? Gin? Tequila? Vodka?"

Humbert orders tequila because the word makes him think of the sun, of a desert, of cactus. A woman with woolen earmuffs going down the street stops for a moment to look at a little Christmas tree, decorated with garlands and tiny balls, in a garbage can. The waiter is already back, serving him the tequila in a small glass. The label on the bottle reads JOSÉ CUERVO. He also leaves him a saucer with a salt shaker and half a lemon, but the mere thought of going through the ritual of licking the salt and sucking on the lemon before drinking down the tequila irritates him beyond expression. He drinks it down and asks for more. The waiter brings another, in another glass, with another piece of lemon. If he asks for many more tequilas, the table will soon be full of half lemons. So why haven't they brought him another salt shaker? He had not consumed the lemon, and they had brought him another. By the same token, he had not used the salt shaker, and they ought to have brought him another. Something is out of whack here, but the effort required to follow the thread of the argument is so tiring that he turns his attention to something that won't require him to think so hard.

He looks at his glass and wonders if those little glasses have a special name. If only he had Hildegarda's dictionary . . . If only, as before (a before whose border blurs in the distance between two and four weeks earlier), he had the energy to jot down on a scrap of paper "Look up synonyms for glass and find the one that corresponds to little glass . . ." He remembers the word "tankard" and finds it stunning. Each glass for each different drink ought to have a different name. Once, making small talk, a waiter had told him the names of a number of glasses: "up glasses," for cocktails served without ice, straight up, like a Manhattan up, or a martini up . . . ; "rock glasses," for cocktails served with ice or water, like whiskey sours, Manhattans, vodka tonics, scotch and water . . . ; "tall glasses," in which Bloody Marys, piña coladas, Tom Collinses, fizzes, and beer must be served . . . ; "cordial glasses," for Kahlua and Amaretto-type liqueurs; brandy snifters, for cognac; "sherry glasses," for Harvey's Bristol Cream . . . When he looks back down at his glass, he doesn't want it any more. He can already predict how it will taste if he brings it to his lips. What a strange feeling, to be repelled by a familiar taste, when till now he had always been nauseated the first time he tried new foods whose taste was unfamiliar!

He looks at the first page of the other two newspapers and pushes them aside. He asks for the check, pays, and just as he is getting up, manages to snatch up the glass and gulp down what's left. But this gesture seems absurdly tragic to him. He gathers up the papers, sticks them under his arm, and goes outside.

He walks under the tress in a square. All at once, just as he had felt, before going into the bar, that, despite its not appealing to him, it was relaxing for the place to be clean and quiet, now the neighborhood seems too bland, too *pretty*. It is a *nice* neighborhood, and he finds this very unpleasant. He throws the paper into the garbage can and breaks into a trot. If only his feelings would take a definite turn instead of this constant fluctuation, this swinging back and forth between desiring and despising . . .

He goes into the first train station he comes across and gets on the first train that comes along, without looking to see which part of the city it's heading for; once inside, he shuts his eyes, trying not even to count the number of stations the train stops at.

•

Two policemen stand close to the turnstiles at the exit. He takes the stairs two at a time. On the street, he walks around among the pimps and the bums. One drunk, soaked with slushy water from the melting snow, is clinging to a parking meter. In a clothing store window all the mannequins are undressed and wigless; some of them are missing arms. A man on top of a ladder is taking down the Christmas lights and signs bearing wishes for a Happy New Year. He walks by two sex shops, tramples already-trampled snow, and slips and almost falls. At the third sex shop, he stops and looks in the window. At the movie theater next door, they're showing *Foxtrot*, a movie they're advertising with enormous billboards containing enlarged reproductions of favorable reviews taken from sex magazines. They include no pictures, suggesting that it has been impossible to choose a single still, as none of them could possibly be put on public display. He keeps on walking. Next door is another sex shop. He goes in.

He comes to a stop in the middle of the room. Only one of the walls is lined with sex toys: rubber vaginas and penises, fantasy condoms, whips, ben wa balls, inflatable boy and girl dolls . . . The other walls, painted yellow, are lined with rows and rows of magazines. On the ceiling there are three fluorescent panels, in one of which two of the tubes are flickering. He finds it odd that the two broken tubes should be precisely in the same panel when (by random chance) the probability of their being in different panels was much greater. This leads him to conclude that there is a defect in the fixture itself. Next to the door, on a platform, a bored elderly man with glasses and long sideburns is leaning on a counter as high as the tops of his clients' heads, overseeing the room, apparently keeping everything under control. Heribert looks at the condoms: there are blue ones, pink ones, green ones, black ones, transparent ones, and red ones . . . They come with bumps, with filaments, one has a little hand with five fingers at the tip, several have protruding stars. The boxes say that these extras give the woman pleasure and make her go mad with delight. The penises are all different sizes, colors, and shapes. Some reproduce the texture, the veins, and the shape of the real thing, but others are perfectly cylindrical, or cylindrical with bumps at the tip, like porcupines . . . They look to him like orthopedic devices. He looks at the magazines. In the first one he opens there are pictures of a man with one woman. In the second, there are two men with one woman. In the third, there are two women. He opens a fourth: two women with one man. The fifth one he opens has two men with one woman again. He opens a sixth: there is a whole slew of people and part of the fun seems to consist of mixing whites, blacks, and Asians, and men and women. In the most general shot, Heribert counts four men and five women. He thinks it's too convoluted to excite anyone.

Farther on is the teenage girl section, most of them unaccompanied, in positions of self-gratification, and in black and white. The magazines of men with men are all in another department, a bit farther on. One of the guys in charge of the store is busy attaching price tags to a pile of inflatable dolls, which, inside their clear plastic bags, look a lot like dead bodies.

The people in the store are mostly middle-aged men. When he entered, he thought he would find more teenagers. The men must be office workers, killing time after work (Heribert looks at his wristwatch; a little after 5:00 P.M.) before going home. There are old men, too, with that defeated look some retired people develop. A guy of about twenty-five is looking at a magazine that shows a woman and a Great Dane.

Heribert continues on, toward the back of the place, where the booths are located, announced by a large neon sign: PEEPSHOW. On the door of each booth hang two pictures and two titles, each of which, respectively, corresponds to one of the two films projected there. He looks at the doors to each of the booths and at each of the titles. By one of the walls next to the first booth there are two video games with Martians, and there's a boy playing at one of them.

He gets change from a machine he spots in the back. He looks at all the doors once again. He has trouble deciding which picture to choose. He goes into the one whose protagonist's face was the prettiest in the photograph.

The space he is enclosed in measures less than a square meter. Against one of the four walls there is a bench. He sits down on it. In front of him is a white surface. On the wall to the right, two machines with slots for coins labeled A and B. He sticks a coin into the slot labeled B. The light in the cabin goes out and the movie appears before his eyes, emerging from a projector (he stands up to get a better look) whose light flows out onto a tilted mirror located over the head of the seated spectator. From the mirror, the image is cast onto the white surface (he touches it: formica). On the screen, two girls (one blonde, one with light brown hair) and a boy (with dark brown hair) appear on a sofa. The boy is wearing a polo shirt (sky blue, with a Lacoste alligator); the girls (one of whom was white and the other black) are wearing stockings and garters (white stockings on the one with the white garters and gold on the one with the black garters) and high-heeled shoes (black for both of them). The boy is penetrating one of the girls, while the other goes from kissing the girl being penetrated, to kissing the boy, to kissing both of their genitals. Heribert quickly realizes that the booth is just isolated enough from the outside so that its occupant (aroused by the film) can masturbate in peace. He looks for traces on the walls, the surface of the screen, the floor set with shiny, irregular, multi-colored tiles, the bench; it's dark, though, so he doesn't find any. When he looks up at the screen again ("What a jerk," he thinks, "I'm missing the movie."), the position of the officiants has shifted: the blond is performing fellatio on the boy as he performs cunnilingus on the brown-haired girl, who is sitting on top of him. At this point, the projection comes to a halt and the light in the booth goes on. Heribert inserts another coin. The action continues. Now the camera focuses, close up, on the activities of the blond girl, until the boy discharges all over her eyes, nose, and lips; she smiles contentedly. The boy and the brown-haired girl are also smiling contentedly. Then there is a brief pause (of only a few seconds), and the same girls appear, now sitting down, all dressed and demure, drinking from tall glasses. One of them moves her lips in silence, as if speaking, and the other nods in agreement as she runs her tongue over her upper lip. The blond girl picks up the receiver and dials a number. The brown-haired girl drinks her drink and smiles. The blonde sits down. A short while later they look at the door with a surprised expression on their faces (conveying the impression that someone has knocked). The brown-haired girl goes to open it and finds the same boy from before at the door, wearing the same polo shirt, but now with pants, carrying a cardboard box the size of a pizza. Gesturing and moving their lips, they invite him in. He comes in. He seems shy. The brown-haired girl takes out her handbag, gives him a five-dollar bill, and searches for change (obviously to give him a tip), but she only comes up with big bills. She looks surprised as the other girl searches through her handbag and also finds no change. Without missing a beat, they get out another glass for the boy, fill it for him, refill their own, and smile at him. He smiles, too, but shyly. The blond unbuttons two buttons on her blouse, gazing at the boy and bending down to flick the ash from her cigarette into the ashtray (suddenly they are smoking; had he not noticed until that moment, or has the cigarette appeared magically?), revealing a good expanse of breast. The brown-haired girl runs her tongue over her lower lip. The boy smiles broadly to indicate that he's understood. He kisses the brown-haired girl, who runs her hand up the boy's leg until she reaches his groin, in exaggerated evidence . . .

The projection breaks off again. He leaves. Another man is leaving another booth at the very same moment, staring at the ground, his face red as a beet. Heribert looks at the man's shoes to see if he has splattered. He thinks he could have put a coin in slot A, to see what it was. He walks out into the street, wondering why he hasn't had an erection the whole time, neither leafing through the magazines nor in the booth.

.

He goes into a state of rapture at a newsstand, looking at the magazine covers. He sees a magazine (*Mademoiselle*) displaying articles on clothing, beauty, health, and love, aimed especially at women and with Brooke Shields's face on the cover. He remembers how, as a boy, he had only had fashion magazines to masturbate to. He buys it. He leafs through it. He feels a foggy twinge of arousal. He goes into the first bar he finds. He sits at the bar. He orders a whiskey. He pays up. He takes a drink. He leafs through the magazine. A woman with very red lips hides her face behind a veil, to promote Revlon lipsticks. A well-known TV actress, with a bottle of Max Factor perfume in her hand, says: "Part of the art of being a woman is knowing when not to be too much of a lady." There is a striped bathing suit, with a tutu, from Saks Fifth Avenue. He finds the model absolutely beautiful. Cacharel, on the facing page, announces a perfume called Anaïs Anaïs (a reference to Anaïs Nin?). On a motorcycle rides a young man in a black jacket and a young woman in a slip, also black, both wearing Carrera glasses. A girl is jogging in Max Factor WaterProof. Dexatrim shows a photograph of Melody Mahoney of Warren (Indiana), who lost 105 pounds in thirty-six weeks by taking one Dexatrim capsule a day. There is also an interview with Michael Caine: "the man women love to love." Another ad for a bathing suit with tutu, by Lakeside. Angie Dickinson reports that California avocadoes have only seventeen calories a slice ("If you take into account," it says in one corner of the ad, "that there are sixteen slices to a medium-sized avocado.") The headline for Sambuca Romana says, "If they try to tell you that Sambuca Romana is an after-dinner drink, tell them you weren't born yesterday. You just look that way." Chimère says: "Chimère perfume: From a distance, it's discreet and elegant; from close up, it's out of this world." The page is split between two shots. On top, a woman at an office desk is surrounded by three men. Underneath, she's embracing one man. (One of the three from the picture on the top? A new one?) He has another drink of whiskey. He heads toward the bathroom.

There is an article on how to stop biting your nails. A girl wrapped in a pink towel says, "I never felt like this until I tried Caress." Caress is a soap. Many pages on how to sunbathe. A long article titled "The Elegant Art of Flirting." A report on dressing in ecological colors. Two girls look out at him from an article titled "Love in the Afternoon," which begins: "Don't wait for the sun to set to put on a sexy dress. We have a series of new designs for you that can be worn all day long . . ." He unzips his pants and begins to fondle himself. What if he were to fall in love with one of those models with almond eyes who look out at him from the ads? Searching for them and finding out whether they were as seductive in the flesh as they are on paper would be a struggle . . . Even to have thought of falling in love with them makes him smile. And yet, he has fallen in love a few times: many years ago . . . Has he really been in love, though, or is it an illusion he half-remembers that doesn't jibe with the dictionary definition of the word? It occurs to him that it must be an arduous task to write a dictionary, to have a precise knowledge of all sentiments and to define them, to know exactly what it is to fall in love, what passion is, where the line between good and evil and between pleasure and perversion falls, or between abundant, numerous, plethoric, overflowing, considerable . . .

He is thinking all of this as he stares at the tiles, the pictures in the magazine long forgotten. He is profoundly bored. He lets go. His erection goes limp and disappears at once. He leaves the magazine on top of the paper towel dispenser, goes back out to the bar, drinks up the third gulp of whiskey, and opens the door to the street.

In the subway, the guy sitting across from him is so odious that he wishes him dead. But he soon cools off. Wishing him dead is too much of an exertion. He looks away from the man and realizes that if he had to describe him without looking he would no longer remember him. This pleases him. When he looks back at him (the flabby face, the fish eyes, the pencil mustache, the idiotic smile . . .), he no longer hates him. He is entirely indifferent to him.

He gets home. Helena is pulling dead leaves off the plants. She tells him they're dying for lack of air and light. If he would only keep them upstairs, in the studio, they'd be better off. But since he refuses . . . She doesn't understand why Heribert has this phobia about plants. In any case, they'll have to move soon, Helena says, and if they decide to leave the city, she'll make sure to find a place with a nice garden and a deck. She also says they'll have to buy another car, because the one they have now won't do for commuting back and forth to the city every day.

Helena has decided that she needs to disconnect a little from work. She's always running around, tying up loose ends, dashing from one meeting to the next . . . By the way, she's met a very interesting young artist, whom she'd like him to meet. Helena has seen what he does, and she thinks it's very exciting. This artist would like to talk with Heribert; she imagines he wants advice. But he seems shy, so she suggests that Heribert be the one to call him the following day, before he takes the car in to the repair shop, which Heribert emphatically refuses to do, saying that since he hasn't used it lately, it's not up to him to take it into the shop.

Helena observes that not only is this affirmation true but it constitutes clear proof that, in fact, Heribert does nothing all day long: he never leaves the house because he has no obligations beyond painting. He could take it into the shop, she goes on, before he starts painting, and this point reminds her that she hasn't asked him how his work has gone that day, nor if he's got a lot done. Her questions go unanswered because Heribert isn't listening: he needs all his powers of concentration to recall that the last time he used the car was about a month and a half ago, when he and Helena went for dinner at Sardi's (and the dinner was lousy), and that when they left, he stained the upholstery with the cognac that spilled from the glass he had taken from the restaurant, hidden in the pocket of his raincoat, before they got mugged while making out in a park. He still has a box of matches from that dinner at Sardi's. He looks for it on the bookshelves. He finds it on a high shelf between a ceramic vase he never liked and a book of cocktail recipes. He looks at it, wondering how many matches there are in a matchbox. It seems evident to him that matchboxes must contain a fixed number of matches. How many, though? Is it, let's say, an exact number, which coincides with some attractive multiple of ten, like fifty or a hundred? Or is it some less elegant multiple of ten, say, sixty or eighty? He considers it inconceivable for the chosen number to be something fussy along the lines of, say, seventy-eight. Of course no one would ordinarily think of counting them, even though, the way things are, you never could tell. What if they cheated and, instead of a hundred matches (if the number of matches meant to fill each box is, indeed, one hundred), they only pack ninety-nine? That would be a gold mine, thanks to the millions of innocent people in the world who buy boxes of matches every day without counting how many there are. And how do they fill the boxes? The image of an endless conveyor belt moving matches along and letting them fall one by one into each box makes him laugh. And how do you make a wooden match? How about a wax match? Suddenly he's very interested in learning how they do it. He remembers a Warner Brothers cartoon he saw on television as a child in which toothpicks were manufactured by cutting down a tree, taking it to the lumberyard, and stripping it of all its excess wood until all that is left is a toothpick, which ends up in a box. Then, they cut down another tree . . .

Helena is standing in front of him, with a scrap of paper in her hand.

"Here. Take it. His name is Humbert. Call him. I told you, he's a little shy, and he won't dare call you. Be nice. I have to go now. (Wow, it's late!)

I'm having dinner with Hipòlita, and I'll be late if I don't run. Big kiss." Heribert sticks the note in his pants pocket and plops into a chair. Since when should he (the, shall we say, established artist who hardly knows how to find the time to work and work in order to maintain the preeminent place he's in) be the one to call the neophyte? In these cases, it's always the one who has more to gain who calls; and the one who has more to gain, in this case, is definitely not Heribert. Still, if Helena is so insistent, it must be someone worthwhile. But he's so shy he doesn't dare to pick up the phone and dial? Or is it that, neophyte and all, he already has a big head? Helena lets the door slam. Heribert falls asleep, strangely certain that he will dream that he awakens after not having had a dream.

He awakens certain of not having had a dream. He thinks of calling Hildegarda to go out to dinner. Then he remembers that he hasn't asked Helena to ask Hipòlita for the Dave Brubeck quartet record.

He's about to call her and ask her to give it to Helena. But just the thought of hearing Hipòlita's voice is too much for him. And if, in addition to hearing her voice, he also has to ask for the record . . . If Helena lent it to her, it's Helena who has to get it back. This is what he'll do: he'll wait a half hour to call Hipòlita's house. That way, when Hipòlita answers, he'll be certain that Helena will have arrived; he will greet Hipòlita briefly (politely, but briefly), and he'll ask to speak with Helena, reminding her that it's about time to ask Hipòlita to return the record.

A half hour later he dials Hipòlita's number, thinking perhaps he's waited too long and they may already have left. As he hears the phone ring on the other end, he thinks to himself that, in point of fact, he could buy another copy of the record and give it to Hildegarda. He's never given her anything. Well, nothing but one of his silkscreens (after she posed for him, a little less than a month ago), but as a gift that seems pretty cheesy. Hildegarda, in contrast, had given him a set of cufflinks set with a dog's head and an old recording of *The Marriage of Figaro* by Marino DelNonno. When he hears Hipòlita's voice answer, he feels like hanging up, but the fear of having to wander through all the record stores in the city looking for such an old record stops him. Hipòlita repeats, "Hello." Heribert decides to speak. He says his name. Hipòlita says it's nice to hear from him. Heribert asks her how things are going. Hipòlita says they're fine and that they should get together soon. Heribert says one of these days, and asks her to put Helena on.

"Helena?"

"Yes, Helena. Weren't you having dinner together?"

"Dinner? Yes! We're having dinner, but . . . she's not here yet and . . ."

It is so obvious that Hipòlita is not expecting Helena for dinner that for a moment Heribert feels like going on with the conversation, forcing her to add facts and details she can't know in order to contrast them later with the facts and details Helena will give him when he subjects her to a similar interrogation. But he prefers to say goodbye to Hipòlita and hang up the phone.

•

As he shaves, his face masked with white soap, Heribert reflects over and over on whether it isn't strange that he's never been jealous. He's never doubted that Helena must be going out with other men. In the end, what does "going out with other men" mean? What does it mean that he goes out with other women? That he embraces another person, caressing her occasionally between sheets that are different from the usual ones? What he finds disconcerting is her telling a lie so flimsy that it falls apart right away. Is Helena having an affair? Of course she is. Who isn't? What is it he finds surprising? That he hasn't ever seen the signs? Why hasn't he ever thought about it before? Is it because he thinks maybe it's too petty to worry about? Or is it because now he's so bored . . . ? "I'm so bored that . . ." As he repeats this phrase he thinks of his easel, and the big white room where he paints, and he sees it all through a very fine dust, gold, or gray, like a fossil.

Whom was she having the affair with? An innocent adolescent? What if it was a tough guy, a sweaty truck driver with a three-day beard? Or a milquetoast? Or a priest? What if it was a girl? A salesman from a clothing store? A Mafia *capo*? What if it was Hug? He bursts out laughing. If it was Hug he'd buy them a bottle of champagne, if only for the show they put on pretending they can't stand each other.

He changes his shoes. He puts on his gray jacket and his black overcoat. Out on the street, he raises his fist to hail a cab. Between the curb and the cab a river of slush is running. The driver opens the door for him. From the curb, Heribert tries to jump into the cab, but his left foot slips and he steps into the slush.

In the restaurant, everyone's having drinks at the bar. Hilari introduces them: Hilda, Herundina, Heribert. Heribert can see that Hilari's after Hilda by the way he takes her arm as they sit. So as he unfolds the napkin before putting it on his lap, Heribert looks at Herundina: she has brilliant eyes and fleshy lips, painted soft red. She has short hair, like so many women this winter, and she's wearing enormous black and white plastic earrings. Hilari says:

"Even if you don't know Herundina, you should recognize her."

The waiter brings the menus and distributes them.

"Why?"

Herundina laughs.

"No," says Heribert. "Why would we know each other, Herundina?"

"It's not that you should know her," Hilari persists, "but you should recognize her. Though I'm not sure you would actually have seen her."

"So why should I recognize you?"

"You used to go out with my sister."

"Don't you see the resemblance?" says Hilari.

"Are you Henrietta's sister?"

"No."

"Heloise's?"

"No, silly. I'm Hannah's sister!"

Any other day, both to break the ice and to try and cover up for the gaffe of mentioning two names that have no connection with her, he would literally have banged his head on the table, which would have made everyone laugh and got the situation flowing to a point that would have allowed for some serious courting. How many times hadn't he seen her! So many. Often, when he had gone to pick Hannah up and once when he had seen the two of them walking down the street together. Any other time, he would have found the perverse detail of going out with the sister of an old girlfriend exciting.

"She had to kill her sister to come to dinner with us today," says Hilari. "She didn't want her to come. When she told Hannah you were going to be here, too, it awakened old passions."

Heribert usually finds Hilari's repartee pretty clever, but today it seems old and tired. How he had always laughed at the guy's constant jokes, his unending stream of lies and stories; now they make him sick. Hilari asks him if something is wrong. He shakes his head. The girl looks at him. Heribert feels incredibly old, and the feeling grows stronger and stronger until, at the end of the meal, he gets up from the table very slowly, hunched over, as if carrying the weight of a century on his shoulders. Hilari thinks he's joking and congratulates him on recovering his good mood. He takes Heribert's arm, takes him aside, and inquires—*sincerely*—as to how he's feeling, and if there's anything wrong. That's what friends are for, he says. He also says that he's been acting distracted and touchy for days, as if he were having problems. He goes on for quite a while about the problem thing, repeats his offer of help, and reminds him that it is precisely in these situations where you discover who your friends are because, often, the very people you thought were irreproachable friends, turn out, when push comes to shove, to be selfish bums incapable of helping someone who would have done anything for them. Heribert stoically puts up with this rant, but when Hilari puts his hand on his shoulder and pats him a few times on the back, he's had enough: he looks him straight in the eye and in all seriousness stamps on his foot with all the strength he can muster.

·

Herundina smiles.

"So . . . ?"

"So what?"

"So what? Oh, nothing. I thought you were going to say something."

"Not me."

"Where would you like to go?"

"Beats me."

"Want to go for a drink?"

"A drink?"

"No, not if you don't want one."

"No, no. A drink would be just fine."

"No, not unless you want one. It's up to you."

"I can't think of anyplace to go."

"I certainly can't. It was you who didn't want to go out dancing with the others."

"Did you want to go?"

"No. I don't care one way or the other. But I thought you had another place in mind."

"Like where?"

"I don't know."

"Well, neither do I."

"Want to go for a walk?"

As soon as he says it, he sees that it's a ridiculous proposition. He doesn't know how to behave. Suddenly he feels entirely unschooled in the art of flirting. He feels as if he had amnesia, as if he were an adolescent again. Worse, because at least as an adolescent he had desire, which egged him on, even though his cheeks always got red and gave him away. What does one do with a woman? Chat her up? If only one could chat without saying anything . . . Or if one could only come up with a fake language, made up of exotic sounds, and say: "Babatoo infrechemina, sadafa nogra ptsu allirà?" And if only she, to all that, were capable of responding, "Troc atodrefa mimenyac! . . ."

He doesn't know how to behave. Should he start kissing her right off and, if she resists, force her right then and there? He seems to remember it doesn't quite go like that. They've been in the taxi for quite a while. They haven't decided where to go, and the driver is showing signs of impatience. Heribert says the first thing that comes into his head:

"Drive straight ahead."

The taxi drives up the avenue. Heribert wonders what to do. Stick his hand under her skirt, right now? Kiss her first? Talk to her about things that will seduce her? How contrived! It all seems hypocritical. In truth, he is so certain (from the way she's looking at him; from the way she agreed not to go dancing with Hilari and Hilda; from the way she's putting up with him, boring as he is; because he can feel it on the surface of his skin) that she likes him as much as he likes her (and realizing this is even more disconcerting) that it all makes him feel even more inhibited.

"You're awfully quiet. Am I boring you?"

He's caught in a bind. To say yes is a lie, and to say no seems ridiculous. The dilemma forces him to choose the middle road: he looks deeply into her eyes, as if he were so much in love that her question was absurd and not deserving of a response. When he can no longer maintain her gaze without betraying its emptiness, he kisses her on the cheek imagining that the girl must consider this style of courting to be senile. How old is this girl? Eighteen, at the most? As long as he doesn't become very aroused, it will be fine. If he manages to look at her coldly, dispassionately, as if contemplating a particularly beautiful porcelain dish, he'll get by. Maybe he should ask what she does. Is she a student? Does she live alone? Does she live with her parents? These are the things one is supposed to ask.

"Are you a student?"

"Yes. Interior design. Did you know that your paintings are perfect for filling up a sparsely furnished space?"

"Oh."

Now what should he do next? He thinks they've gone quite far up the avenue. He tells the driver:

"Turn right at the next corner, and keep driving straight ahead."

He looks at the girl again. She studies interior design.

"Do you work? I mean, do you have a job somewhere as a decorator?"

"Yes, with my father. My father is an interior decorator. Don't you remember? My father: Hannah's father."

"Oh. Of course."

He has absolutely no recollection of what Hannah's father did for a living.

"Do you live with your parents?"

"No, I live with my mother. My parents are divorced and now I live with Mom. I see Dad in the studio whenever I go to work there."

How do eighteen- and twenty-year-olds behave nowadays? Do they have the same attacks of shyness that he had, fifteen years ago? The taxi is still driving straight ahead; if he keeps going much farther they'll end up right in the water.

"Listen," the driver says, "if I keep going straight we'll end up right in the water."

Heribert tells him to turn right, and go down the avenue. He suddenly feels very tired. He decides to wrap things up: he asks Herundina for her phone number. She gives it to him, in exchange for his. He promises to phone her.

"Please do. I'd like very much to see what you're painting now."

He leaves her at the door to her mother's house. What must she look like now? He remembers her from a few years back when he picked Hannah up at home. Every so often while he was in bed with the daughter he would fantasize about the mother.

Then the taxi starts up and takes him home. Heribert pays the driver, who has a sympathetic look on his face, for which Heribert gives him an excessive tip, so that he will realize that if either of them should feel sympathy for the other, it is he for the driver. At home, in the bedroom, he hears the door as he's undressing. Helena. He hurriedly shuts off the light, gets into bed, and pretends to be asleep.

H eribert looks at the new, totally blank, canvas he's placed on the easel. He's put the paint, brushes, and solvents on a small table. He runs his hand over his cheek. What if, really and truly, he cannot paint another stroke, never again? In his current state of mind, even to entertain a doubt about it seems a sign of valor. This gives him confidence. But when he touches the canvas with the charcoal pencil, he doesn't know what to draw. Downstairs the phone rings twice. Helena picks it up. He hears her speak: it is such a distant whisper that he wouldn't be at all surprised if he had to take a train, a subway, and a bus to get downstairs.

To break the spell, all he has to do is yawn. When he was a child he would endow some gesture with an shamanic power, so that he would get what he was wishing for if he carried out the ritual, like tracing three circles over his belly before going into the classroom where he had to take an exam. He yawns halfheartedly.

Helena calls out to him.

"I'm going shopping. I'll be back later."

I'll be back "later"? One is always back "later" when one goes out. Later than what, then? Wouldn't it make more sense to have said, "I'll be right back?" Of course she will buy something so as not to come back empty-handed, but what he's sure about is that she's not "going shopping."

He hears the front door close. He quickly puts on his jacket and coat, leaves the brushes dirty and the paints uncovered, and goes down the stairs.

Once in the street, he's taken aback: he doesn't see her anywhere. Then he spots her off in the distance: one very blond head among all the others. He picks up the pace. He runs until she's a reasonable distance ahead. Then he thinks that that distance isn't, in fact, very reasonable.

He slows down. He thinks: "Now I'll find out who her lover is. Now this is something I find interesting." But in his heart of hearts he realizes that it doesn't really interest him all that much, and he's sorry. In truth, he doesn't really care if he never learns what the guy who's *going out* with Helena looks like, how he dresses, whether or not he's a nice guy. Helena turns a corner. Heribert follows her.

•

Carrying three shopping bags, Helena takes the same path in reverse. Heribert follows her at a distance. She's gone to a pastry shop, a boutique, and a bookstore, and she spends so little time in each place that it would be impossible for her to have been with a lover, no matter how efficient the two of them might have been.

Helena searches in her coat pocket for the keys. Heribert watches her from a distance, and when he sees her go in, he goes for a walk so as not to get home right away. He wonders whether to go into a bar. He does. It's half empty, with wooden paneling and mirrors. Not exactly dark, but lacking in light. He sits down on a barstool, leans on the bar, and when it's time to order he remembers that not so long ago (today? yesterday? he doesn't feel like wracking his brain to remember exactly when) he had had trouble in another, different, bar choosing what to drink when the time came. He doesn't want the situation to repeat itself now, so when the bartender asks him what he'll have, he looks for something to latch on to. When he sees the beer taps, he feels he's been saved.

"Draft beer. A pint."

Later on, when he spies the whisky bottles aligned before the mirror facing him (there is a mirror directly in front of him: he's been seeing his face reflected in it for a while and hasn't recognized himself until now), he thinks that if he had seen them first he would have ordered whisky. The waiter serves him the pint. He pays up. He licks off the foam.

•

Heribert opens the door to the house and goes in. Helena is in the kitchen, and she looks up from the carrots she's chopping.

"I didn't know where you were."

"I went out for a walk. I didn't think you'd be back for lunch."

"What about you, are you eating at home today?"

"Yes."

As she prepares the carrots and spinach, Heribert cleans the mushrooms and celery. The morning call must have been Hipòlita, he figures, to warn Helena that he had called last night and she hadn't known how to answer the questions she wasn't expecting. Could Helena have thought it didn't matter? If she has spoken with Hipòlita, she must imagine he has suspicions. Why doesn't she come up with a lie so good he'll even have to doubt his own suspicions? Or doesn't she care? Or does she think that she doesn't have to cover things up? And why hasn't she asked him what he's been working on today? With every hour that goes by he sees more clearly that either he has to begin painting, without stopping, and with an energy that clearly he neither possesses nor desires to create, or when the day comes to hang the canvases, he won't have a single one, and he will not be opening a single bottle of champagne at a single opening.

·

"You know what?" says Helena as they peel oranges. "I went to the theater with Hester yesterday, and we saw a show that was so good that even you, who claim not to like theater, and never want to go, even you . . ."

He's put off by the way she's pulled Hester out the hat to let him know that she didn't go with Hipòlita. It's as if she were taking him for a fool. Heribert supposes that now Helena is waiting for him to say, "Hester? Weren't you going out with Hipòlita?" And then she would say, "Hipòlita? No." And then if he continues to question her, she will act surprised and say, "Did I say I was going with Hipòlita? I meant Hester." Considering how clever Helena is, he can even foresee a more detailed ending, to make it more believable. "I always slip and mix up one name for another, and I say Hester when I mean Hipòlita or Hipòlita when I mean Hester. I do it all the time." But Heribert has another idea: not to act surprised at all, and calmly to ask her, "Oh, what did you see?" If she doesn't realize he's caught her in a lie when he says this, at least she'll be intrigued. Or does she think he's forgotten the whole episode? Or believed the story? It's no use calling

Hester on some pretext and subjecting her to subtle questioning because she'll have been tipped off that she is last night's alibi. What outcome is he really interested in? Not knowing what to say, and not yet having said anything, he sets the knife and the peeled orange on the table, gets up from the chair, and says he's going to the bathroom.

·

He lines up all the blank canvases he has in the studio and examines them. What if he showed just that: white canvases, without the slightest trace of a human hand? It's been done. Minimalism. And anyway, if he signs them he will have placed a few strokes of his own. He could not sign them. Someone must have done that, too. Is there anything original left to do? Even halfheartedly filling up all the walls of an exhibition isn't new. Do you really have to do something new? Why? What is more important, to be honest or to be original? Out of honesty, people often refused to be original. And out of honesty people often fall silent rather than open their mouths only to hear their own voices. Will he be able to tell when he opens his mouth and nothing interesting comes out?

Helena's voice floats up to him:

"I'm leaving. See you later."

It seems to him that, in the past, she would always tell him where she was going when she left, to the gallery or to do this or that, or to see this or that person. Or maybe she had never done anything of the sort, and now he just imagined she had. He hears the front door close. He puts on his jacket, and as he goes down the stairs he tries to calculate how many times he's done that this year. On the table next to the door there are two brochures: one from Chevrolet and another from Ford.

This time he has no trouble spotting her. She's standing in front of the windows of a shoe store. Heribert hangs back by a telephone booth and watches her out of the corner of his eye. There's a drunk hanging onto a mailbox, and a girl (dressed like an old-fashioned secretary) is trying to mail a big stack of letters (and looking afraid that the drunk may attack her). The phone in the phone booth rings. Heribert looks at Helena, who's still looking at shoes, but has gone on to another window. He's afraid the constant ringing of the phone no one is answering will make her turn around. He goes into the booth, picks up the receiver, and says hello. On the other end, he doesn't hear a thing: no breathing, no click to indicate the call has been cut off. The line was totally dead. He hangs up and turns around. Helena is walking down the street. "All this," he thinks, "just to see her go shopping or to the gallery . . ." Helena signals, and a taxi jumps three lanes and stops right in front of her. Heribert has to stop another one, quickly, but feels ridiculous lifting his arm to flag it down. He will feel even more ridiculous, once inside, when he has to say, like in the movies, "Follow that car." He remembers one where a taxi driver is thrilled when they ask him to follow another car, saying that he had been waiting all his long working life for that moment, like in the movies.

When he is in the cab and says it, the driver looks at him in the rearview mirror, gives a short laugh, and starts to talk. He talks nonstop the whole time, recklessly passing the other cars. Once, when Helena's driver jumps a red light, Heribert's steps on the gas and (between two lanes of traffic, almost scraping the cars on either side) shoots forward and crosses the street on the red just as a Cadillac Seville coming from the left makes the turn. They make such headway that, by the next red light, Heribert's taxi is directly behind Helena's. Heribert hides behind the driver's head. If they keep up this pace, he thinks, soon they'll take the lead, leaving the other car in their wake, turning this into the most original chase in history, in which they precede the pursued car instead of following it. They go across the bridge.

Fifteen minutes later, Helena's taxi stops on a wide, solitary avenue, lined with houses.

"Park across the street, a little farther down."

Having to come up with such stratagems exhausts him. The driver says something under his breath and smiles. Looking out the back window, Heribert watches as Helena gets out of the cab and goes into one of the houses.

•

A couple of children are playing with an enormous ball in one of the yards. Heribert tries unsuccessfully to figure out what they're playing: sometimes it looks like soccer, then like baseball, then a minute later like handball. Then they laugh and take a rest, leaning on the fence. Once, he thinks they look at him, whisper about him, and laugh again.

He sits on the curb, and since he's getting bored, he starts doing things. First he counts the seconds that elapse between one particularly loud shout from one of the kids and the first car to go down the street (another taxi): 634. Then he counts the minutes until the next car (a Mercury Cougar) goes by: 18. He adds the 634 seconds and the 18 minutes: 652. He finds it interesting to add up dissimilar things. In school they said you couldn't add apples and oranges. If he adds the 652 to the 2 kids playing in the yard, he gets 654 seconds, minutes, and kids. He counts the cars parked on that stretch of street: 17. Added to the previous 654 that makes 671 seconds, minutes, kids, and cars on that stretch of street. He thinks of adding in the 4 stoplights, the two garbage cans he can see, the fire hydrants, the potholes. If he could add up all objects, all feelings, all ideas, all creatures, add them all up together, everything would be so simple. How easy it would be to face any situation, get out of any labyrinth, form a fairly accurate image of the world; the world (for example) would be exactly 78,345,321,834,042,751,539 things. If he could just diagram this feeling of perplexity! But how? Turning the canvas into a blackboard and writing down all those figures seems idiotic to him. And the mere thought of coming up with a more elaborate way to depict that morass wears him out.

He lets himself fall back. It feels wet. He looks at the white sky. It's cold out. He thinks it's strange that the two children are playing outside on such a cold day. He thinks, "If I start to imagine that the sky is empty, I'll fall upwards, I'll fall into the clouds."

After a wait that seems interminable, Helena appears arm in arm with a tall man, with brown hair and a broad mouth, wearing a very long, gray raincoat and glasses with apple green, almost fluorescent, frames.

Thinking that he has to get up to follow them, he lies down again and keeps trying to convince himself that gravity will suck him up into the sky, but he doesn't quite manage to believe it. When Helena and her escort catch a cab at the corner, he gets up, brushes off his pants, and starts walking home.

•

He opens the door, turns on the light in the foyer, and then, one by one, he turns on all the lights in all the rooms of the house. Upstairs, he turns on the light in the studio, and the radio, as he gazes with infinite estrangement upon all the cans, paintbrushes, portfolios, pencils, canvases, and easels. He goes back downstairs. He turns on the other radio, the television, the record player, and leaves them all at full blast. He can't turn on the radio and the cassette player at the same time because turning one on automatically turns the other off. This annoys him. He will never again fall for one of these outlandish models that claim to be a radio and a cassette player at the same time; at the moment of truth they cannot be both radio and cassette player at the same time, and hence it is a lie. He remembers that he has a small transistor radio, which must be in some corner of the house. He looks through all the rooms, until he finds it next to the picnic baskets. He also turns it on. In the kitchen, he turns on all the burners, the oven, the toaster, the blender, the coffee grinder, the mixer. For a moment he's afraid the circuit breaker will blow. He puts the teakettle on the stove, with a little water. The whistle soon joins all the other cries, songs, melodies, conversations, noises, and lights that fill the house. He feels at home, in a house full of life. He goes out to the door, opens it, and keeps pressing the buzzer over and over again. The din produced by all those appliances working at once is delightful. "If in this precise moment the telephone rang, I'd be a truly happy man." He could phone a friend and ask him to call, but that would ruin the fun.

Just then the phone rings. He listens for a good while, one more sound among all the screeches, squawks, and whistles bubbling up from every corner of the house. Then he thinks maybe he should answer. He stops ringing the doorbell, closes the door, and picks up the telephone. He can't hear a thing over the racket. At the top of his lungs he asks the person on the other end, whom he isn't able to identify, to give him a moment, and one by one he shuts off the record player, the radio, the cassette, the toaster, the lights, the blender, the burners, the oven, the transistor radio, until the house is plunged into absolute silence and darkness. He sits on the floor and feels his way (because his eyes, dazzled by the previous brilliance, take a while to adjust to the absence of light) over to the telephone. It's Herundina, who asks him what all the ruckus was. Heribert tries to explain, and when the girl seems to have understood, he is surprised because not even he understands it very well; he even has to ask her to repeat the question, "What are you doing this evening?" because he hasn't the foggiest notion what he's doing that night or what he ought to answer.

•

He has taken off his wristwatch and placed it on the table in front of him. For fifteen minutes (when he's already been waiting a half hour) he has silently been following the progress of the second hand. He has interrupted this contemplation three times, each time to order more rum. Now the waiter is filling his glass again. He takes a swallow and quickly goes back to studying the second hand. He is surprised to have lived so many years with watch hands before him and never to have been aware of the obsessive life they led. Now he perceives them all, the agile second hand, the slow minute hand, and the lumbering hour hand, as unsung comrades. He kisses the face of the watch.

He's disconcerted at Herundina's not yet having arrived. What if it's all his imagination, and she hasn't called and, consequently, they haven't arranged to meet at all? What if he dreamed it and now, in a waking state, he is fruitlessly awaiting a meeting that will never take place? Or what if he's dreaming now and fretting about a date that can't take place unless he wakes up? He feels so disinclined to think about the possible reasons why the girl hasn't shown up that, when he finishes the last glass of rum, he gets up, pays the bill, leaves the restaurant, and heads down the street.

A few steps farther on, he leans against a telephone booth, waiting for a taxi. Three of them go by, all occupied. The fourth, also occupied, stops in front of the restaurant and, to Heribert's surprise, Herundina gets out, smoothes out her leopard-print miniskirt, unwraps a piece of gum, and puts it in her mouth. For a moment, Heribert considers going back into the restaurant, running into her, scolding her a bit for arriving late, accepting whatever excuses she offered, sitting down at a table with her, and searching for things to talk about over dinner, only to find himself at a loss as to what to do with her afterwards. When the taxi she had gotten out of starts up and the signal light goes on, Heribert hails it, opens the door, and gets in, with time enough to watch through the rear window as Herundina pushes open the restaurant door.

When he walks into the bedroom at home he is surprised to find Helena already there, asleep. It's been days since she has beaten him home! As he gets undressed and into bed, he wonders if she is pretending to be asleep, as he has so often done.

A weak sun shines in through the picture window, outlining the contours of things, bringing them into relief in a way that disturbs Heribert, who is sitting on a stool before a canvas, his head resting on the hand of the arm whose elbow is propped on his thigh. On the ground lies a torn canvas. He can hardly believe that just five minutes ago he stomped it to pieces. On the calendar he calculates how many days are left until the opening. Eighteen. He can do twenty paintings in three days, if he wants to. All he needs is a bit of will and a little courage. Has be become so demanding that he no longer approves of work that just months before would have satisfied him? Maybe that's it. Maybe, two days before the show, the pressure will make him prolific. It wouldn't be the first time that urgency had made him prolific. Maybe in the end it's just that he isn't anxious enough yet, and the calm was boring him. Maybe if he tries now . . . He picks up the charcoal pencil. He touches the tip of it to the surface of the canvas. He keeps it there for a while, struggling mightily to make even a stroke. Not a single one. He lowers his arm in exhaustion. He sits down in a chair, gasping for air, so tired he thinks he won't be able to do another thing for the rest of the day.

He looks out the window. He moved into this house about a year ago. He chose to work by that window because of all the light it gave him. For almost a year now, he has been there each day, painting, and observing the turn-of-the-century brick building across the street when he takes a break. The first figure to become familiar was a young man who lived on the third floor. At first he had been surprised to see him at the window so often. He soon understood that the guy was pacing, along one invariable route: He walks purposefully from one end of the room to the window and, once there, stops, looks out at the street, turns on his heel, and walks back to the other end of the room . . . Over and over, for the space of a minute, for minutes on end, for an entire hour, all morning and all afternoon, every day of every week of every month. For how many years?

In time, Heribert has come to recognize all his sweaters. He has one very loud one, yellow and blue, and he seems happier on the days he wears it. In the summer, Heribert has seen all his t-shirts. Once, at the peak of August, he saw him in a bathing suit. He often smokes a pipe as he paces. Sometimes he pretends to read a book. Once he stayed at the window for a long time, hugging a record cover to his chest. Often, when the window is open, he shouts things down to people on the street. Heribert has only seen him outdoors once, on his way home with two older women. He was on the corner, arguing with a lamppost. Now he is at home, going through his daily paces. How many miles must he clock in a year? "Crazy as he is," thinks Heribert, "any minute now he could take a shot at me. Maybe even the next time around!" He can see him now, approaching the window as he always does, but this time he's not holding a book, or a pipe, or a record cover, but a revolver, which he aims at Heribert. As he pictures this, Heribert closes his eyes, the better to imagine that perhaps at this precise moment the guy is aiming a gun at him. "What will I do if he shoots and misses?" Would he throw himself to the ground? Could he go on living there, knowing that the madman might attack again? Would this finally force him to look for a new apartment or, more to Helena's liking, a house in the suburbs? How exhausting, though.

Heribert opens his eyes again and sees the guy pacing the room, coming up to the window, and looking out, as always. He hears the phone ring, hears Helena pick up the receiver, hears her say it's for him. He picks up the phone. Helena hangs up the other extension. Heribert leans up against the window, certain that, as always, nothing will happen. It's starting to snow. Herundina is apologizing for having been late for their date the day before. A meeting. Do twenty-year-olds have meetings? Herundina says it had to do with school. She asks if he waited long.

"Two minutes. When you didn't show up after two minutes, I left."

"You could have waited a little longer."

"What for, if you didn't get there for another hour and fifteen minutes?"

"How do you know, if you weren't there? I don't get it."

If he were a writer, he would write about fear of the blank page . . . Maybe he could paint something like that. A painter in front of an easel with an empty canvas? An empty canvas painted white?

"I don't think you're listening to me," Herundina breaks in.

"Sure I'm listening."

"You're very strange."

Heribert hears Helena say she's going out. He thinks, "Who did she think this was on the phone?" He starts making excuses into the receiver. Says he has to leave right away, promises to phone, accepts her apology for being late the night before, agrees to her being the one to call, on Wednesday, hangs up the phone, picks up his coat.

·

This time, the wait is more tedious. It doesn't amuse him to count the parked cars, the time elapsed between the passing of two cars, the potholes, the windows of a house, the windows of all the houses on the street, the trees in the yards, the trees that grow on the sidewalks, the number of the house Helena went into . . . And the children aren't there, either, perhaps because snow is falling softly the whole time. With his lapels up high and wearing a wide-brimmed hat (when he saw that the snow was sticking, he picked up a hat; could that bit of precaution be a sign of recovery?), Heribert sits on the curb, thinking that if he's there much longer they'll find him under a good layer of snow, turned into a snowman, a sculpture for the show that will be opening on the twenty-second. From the time Helena goes into the house until the time she comes out, accompanied by greenglasses, exactly two hours, forty-eight minutes, and nine seconds elapse. As he follows them, he turns the hours into minutes in his head. He has been waiting 168 minutes and nine seconds. He turns the minutes into seconds: 10,080, which (with the nine remaining seconds) comes to a total of 10,089 seconds. The snowstorm is thinning.

The couple stops at a corner. Heribert also stops, acting nonchalant. He pulls his hat down over his ears. If they hail a taxi now, he'll really be screwed, because in that neighborhood it will be hard to find another one right away. If the man has a car parked nearby, he'll be in the same fix.

And, even if he's lucky and finds a cab, he feels nauseated at the mere thought of telling another cab driver, "Follow that car."

It has stopped snowing. Helena and glasses were strolling along, laughing, their arms around each other. Heribert thinks that when he gets home he'll have to get the operator to tell him the name of the person who lives at that house number. But, what if the phone is in someone else's name? Or he doesn't have a phone? The couple stops from time to time for a kiss. Heribert pretends to be checking out a shop window or waiting for a bus, sinking lower and lower into his lapels and hat. If only he had a disguise . . . He realizes he's in front of a drugstore with wigs in the window. He rapidly calculates his chances of losing them if he stops for, say, fifteen seconds, to make a purchase. Impossible: they are right at the beginning of the block and there isn't another corner for at least a minute. He goes into the shop and orders the big blonde wig with the curls; he pays; he tells them not to wrap it, takes off his hat, puts on the wig, puts the hat on over it, and goes out, indicating with a gesture to the salespeople and the two customers that they shouldn't follow him out, which of course they do immediately, ignoring his pleas in their amazement.

The couple has progressed as far as Heribert had predicted. He speeds up until he is once more maintaining the distance he considers ideal. "The trouble with amateur detectives," he thinks, "is that they think they'll blend in by acting mysterious. But no one would ever think of shadowing someone wearing such an outrageous blonde wig." He thinks it's precisely because he looks so outlandish that they will never realize he's trailing them.

On the verge of passing by an optician's shop, he stops for a second, just long enough to size up the situation and buy a pair of sunglasses with pink frames and heart-shaped lenses. In another window he sees a big red-and-white-striped beach ball, next to an ad for suntan lotion that must have been there since summer. They would give the ball as a gift, it said, to anyone who bought a bottle of the lotion. He finds it so perfectly logical (that they give you a beach ball for buying a bottle of lotion) that he feels they needn't even have advertised it. The world should always be like that: if you buy a dress, they should give you a typewriter; if you buy a cookbook, they should give you a hockey stick . . . He goes into the store, buys the tanning lotion, and asks for the ball.

"It's not very useful for skiing," the owner jokes, as he eyes the wig in a way he thinks is inconspicuous. He wraps up the lotion and gives Heribert the ball, in a plastic bag.

Heribert doesn't answer. He runs out with the bottle of lotion in his coat pocket. He throws the plastic bag on the ground and tries to bounce the ball. Since it doesn't bounce at all in the snow, he walks along throwing it up in the air and bouncing it off his head. The ball bounces weakly off the hat. A few people stop to stare at him. Not everyone, though, which he finds disconcerting at first, until he reasons that, in fact, it was more logical not to. Why should anyone turn around? He walks past a door in which he can see his reflection. He takes a good look at himself: with those heart-shaped pink glasses, that enormous curly wig, and that beach ball in his hand, he made the perfect shadow. Maybe he could start a new life as a detective. If he could just work up the courage to start over from scratch, doing . . . whatever . . . He looks closer. Something is missing, something loud: maybe some yellow shoes, plastic ones. Where to get them, though, without losing the couple? If he wants to be a success in this trade, he'll have to improve his technique. He'll have to put on a different disguise at every corner. On this block, a fat lady with a dachshund. On the next one, a pirate, with a striped shirt, a bandana, a five-day beard, an eye patch, and a hook for a hand. On the next, an astronaut, eating a lemon ice. And on the next, a tiger with a top hat . . . The world was so far from perfection! A little girl passing by points at him. She laughs and pulls on the arm her father was holding her hand with. Heribert lifts his leg as if to give her a good kick. The little girl's laughter makes many of the passersby turn around, including Helena and her companion. Helena and Heribert look straight at each other, and he is afraid she will recognize him. If she does, he's lost. Heribert's and Helena's eyes meet for an instant, with an intensity that makes him think that not even the dark glasses can keep her from recognizing him. "My eyes," he thinks. "I should have masked my eyes!" After an unbelievably long second, Helena and glasses smile and go on walking. They hadn't recognized him! They'd taken him for an eccentric, a madman! He is so pleased he almost runs up to Helena and her companion and takes each of them by the arm to share the joke with him. If they were real people—and not just flesh puppets—they would laugh with him and all three of them would go home, and while four-eyes went to bed with Helena, he would paint thirty paintings in an hour. And then they'd all go out for drinks.

In another window he sees some really baggy pants with a floral print: just the touch he was missing. He goes in, asks for the biggest size they have, pays, says no to a box or a bag, and puts them on right then and there, on top of the ones he's already wearing. He looks at himself in a mirror: the effect can no longer be improved upon. Playing with the ball, he goes out into the street, not bothering to warn the salespeople (on whose faces he can read the need to break the monotony of the workday by following his progress from the doorway) to stay inside.

Once outside, though, Helena and her escort are nowhere to be seen. He starts to run. Maybe they've turned the first corner. He doubts they could have gotten so far in the short time he's been inside. Just as he thought. They aren't on the side street, neither left nor right. He goes back. Maybe they've gone into a store. But there are no more stores on that side of the street. On the other side, though, are a fish market and a bar. He crosses the street, with the ball in his arms. He has been too cocky. They're not in the fish market: he can see that from the street, through the clear plate glass. He opens the door to the bar. Indifferent to the gaping of the two winos propped up on the bar, and to the shouts of the owner (who is showing him the door with the index finger of his left hand), he looks the place over and sees that they aren't there. He goes outside. They are nowhere in sight. They can't have disappeared just like that, unless (now he sees it, as soon as he turns the other corner, and he looks with hatred at the pole announcing the bus stop) they're on that bus which he can still see in the distance.

In front of his house, as he pays the fare, the driver asks him if this is where they're having the costume party.

"Yes. We're having Mardi Gras a month early and Halloween about two months late. It's like a sort of equator between the two events. One must always try to find the happy medium."

As if he could reinforce his words by doing so, Heribert gives him a splendid tip. Leaving the man gaping makes him feel good. Except for the error of losing his prey, the afternoon has been an unexpected success: Helena's not recognizing him has made him so happy that he claps as he goes into the house. He gets undressed in the foyer and puts the disguise away in a paper bag in the junk closet. In the bathroom he fills the tub with moderately hot water and gets in. He goes under, counting how long he can stay there without coming up for air: one minute, ten seconds.

W hen he hears her arrive, at 5:35 A.M., he pretends to be sleeping, as always. At nine, the alarm goes off. Helena gets up right away. Heribert opens one eye and sees her, sitting on the bed, stretching. How does she manage to sleep so little and not feel the effects? He closes the one eye when he sees that Helena is turning around to wake him up.

"Heribert. It's nine o'clock."

He continues to pretend to be asleep. He hears her get up and shower. He watches her get dressed, on the sly: panties, stockings, bra, blouse, skirt, jacket, shoes. She is a very beautiful woman. Until not so long ago, he could spend hours (maybe not quite hours, but certainly minutes) looking at her eyes, her lips, her eyebrows. Helena picks up her handbag and, before leaving, walks over to him again.

"Lazybones, it's ten o'clock."

A moment later he hears her close the door. He yawns, takes over the middle of the bed, stretches out comfortably, and buries his head in the pillows.

He lifts his head and looks at the clock: 11:30. He feels tired. He stays awake until 2:00, when he falls asleep. At 3:23 the phone rings. He fumbles around on the night table. He thinks he's crushed something hard. A cockroach? He finally finds the telephone. He picks it up. Whenever he happens to think about cockroaches, afterwards, for quite a while, he can't get them out of his head. Now he's afraid they'll start coming out of the holes in the receiver and run into his ear.

It was Hildegarda. What was going on, why hadn't he called her? They make a date. They arrange for Heribert to stop by at 7:00 to pick her up.

He hangs up the telephone and decides to stay in bed until it's time. He sets the alarm for 6:00.

When the clock goes off, he curses at it. He is so definitively not in the mood to get up that he decides to stay in bed a little longer. To watch the minutes tick by, sees 6:15 come and go, then 6:26, 6:30, 6:37, 6:45, 7:00, 7:15, 7:30 . . .

He lies there the whole time with his eyes open, staring at the face of the clock. At 7:45 the phone rings again. It's Hildegarda. Did he fall asleep? Heribert is about to tell her, "I am just not in the mood to get up . . ." but he doesn't, perhaps not wanting to annoy her. Not saying it, though, makes him feel like a coward. Then he thinks maybe it's not so much that he doesn't want to hurt Hildegarda's feelings as that he's just not in the mood even to speak. This new line of reasoning gives him momentary satisfaction. He gets up slowly. He finds that getting up slowly is good. Slowly he gets dressed. Then, he slowly thinks that he hasn't showered. On the verge of wondering why he has to shower he manages not to finish the thought. He undresses slowly. He showers slowly. He dries himself off slowly. He closes the front door slowly. Slowly he raises his arm to hail a cab, which, in Heribert's opinion, approaches too quickly. With measured words he tells the drives to take him to the address as slowly as he can: there is no hurry. When Hildegarda gives him a kiss, he returns it in the slowest of slow motions.

"What's up, are you rusty?"

•

Slowly he sits in a pink armchair, and in absolutely no hurry, he tells Hildegarda that he no longer feels any passion for Helena, nor for painting, nor perhaps for anything at all. (As he tells her this he thinks, with satisfaction, that this decisive declaration of his state of mind, completely at odds with the impassivity of that day in bed, is just what Hildegarda expected to hear from his lips. He vows to himself that from this moment on he will do only what is expected of him.) What if Hildegarda takes him seriously? Will she be capable of asking him if he also feels no passion for her? If she does, he'll slap her in the face, for . . .? For what? For being banal and predictable. But she doesn't ask. At first, this gives him some satisfaction. "Maybe we're cut from the same cloth." Gradually, though, he sees that this possibility doesn't appeal to him either. He's the one who's ill at ease with everything. Annoyed at the possibility that she might be as detached as he, he tells her that Hug has told him about her, about their going out together and, as she can see, all of this was neither here nor there to him. He thinks, "If she gets angry now, or pissed off at my lack of sensitivity in telling her, or if she goes off on Hug for spilling the beans, then I win." She walks over to him and asks him if he'd like to know how they did it. Then she puts her arms around him; they fall to the floor and roll around; she pulls off his pants and pulls up her skirt, stroking him and laughing. Heribert laughs, too, for a moment. He remembers how, before, the smoothness of Hildegarda's cheek used to arouse him to the point of turning into a beast, an athlete. He touches her cheek, hoping to feel that velvety softness again, and even though he feels *that velvety softness* again, it doesn't seem the same. He caresses her clitoris as if barely touching it, and she smiles, giving in to the pleasure. A short while later, though, Heribert yawns, closes his eyes, progressively decreases the friction, and falls asleep.

·

When he awakens he sees Hildegarda, dressed in black, sitting in the pink armchair he had previously occupied. She is looking at him. With severity? With indifference? As if she didn't see him? With disparagement? With curiosity? All those questions strung together, muses Heribert, could be the lyrics to a torch song. How exactly is she looking at him?

"Shall we go out?" she says.

Heribert slowly gets dressed. Does he feel better than before? Worse? "If only I had felt a little guilty . . ." he thinks, but then wonders, guilty of what? If only he could say that Hildegarda was punishing him with indifference, punishing him with contempt . . .

They say goodbye outside. Hildegarda gives him an icy kiss on the lips. Heribert walks away, crossing to the alternate side of the street at every corner.

When he gets home, Helena is arriving at the same time. At the street entrance, they look at each other, each with key in hand, grinning at each other, like tacit accomplices.

"Good evening . . ."

"Good evening . . ."

Pleasantly, they say "after you" on the way in and "after you" at the stairs. This is the first time they have run into each other at night, each coming home separately. At the door to the apartment, the double keys are repeated and the double smiles. "We seem symmetrical." If only symmetry could be applied to everything . . . They take their coats off at the same time, one next to the other, and one next to the other they hang them on two hooks of the coat rack. They brush their teeth in neighboring sinks, symmetrically: one holds the toothbrush with the right hand, and the other with the left. They get undressed at the same time, on either side of the bed. They pick up the top sheet at the same time and get in at the some moment. Heribert wishes they would dream the same dream.

•

Helena wakes him up, hands him the telephone, and disappears into the living room. It's Herundina. Half asleep, he answers, agrees to see her that evening, arranges the time and place, hangs up, thinks that it's the second time Helena has heard Herundina's voice, and goes back to sleep.

A short time later, Helena wakes him up again. She covers the mouthpiece of the telephone with her hand. It's that young man, she says, whom Heribert is supposed to have called and hasn't. Since Helena has called him about seeing some etchings, why doesn't he take a moment and talk to him? He talks to him. Humbert is a painter, he wants to meet him, show him his work, ask for his advice. They arrange to meet that evening. He would stop by Heribert's for a chat and a drink. Heribert estimates that this will leave enough time for him to meet up later with Herundina. He hangs up.

He admits to himself that he's incapable of going back to sleep. He gets up. Helena is having breakfast in the kitchen. She stops her toast and marmalade in mid-air and asks him what he thought of Humbert and what arrangements they had made, and before Heribert can answer, she comes out with a string of praise for this up-and-coming young artist. Heribert, washing his hands in the sink, lowers his head and places it under the flowing water of the faucet in such a way that he manages not to hear a word she is saying.

•

When Helena leaves, he doesn't feel like following her again. He goes back and forth about whether to go up to the studio, but he's afraid of finding himself in front of the blank canvases. And who did Helena think Herundina was?

He was pleased to have had three such different thoughts in such a short time, and he makes an effort to have another one right away, but he can't. When he's about to give up, he sees the telephone: he has to call information and, tactfully, under reasonable pretenses, get the names of the tenants in the building where Helena's young friend lives, to see who he might be. But it sounds like too much trouble for nothing. He sits down to watch TV. He sees one ad for cosmetics, another for cereal, another for toys, another for a health club, another for ladies' underpants, another for a condominium, another for soup, another for yogurt, another for romance novels, another for a razor for legs and underarms, another for bras, another for pants, another for insurance, another for convertible sofas, another for shoes, another for an electric shaver for legs and underarms, another for soft drinks, another for chicken, another for a numismatist. This one, in particular, catches his attention because it claims that while coin collecting is fun, it is also an investment. That's it: maybe what he needs is to find an obsession like coin collecting. Collecting . . . And not just coins, stamps must also fulfill the two objectives. He searches in the yellow pages for the listings of numismatists and philatelists; he tears the pages out, folds them carefully, puts them in his pants pocket, puts on his coat, opens the door, and goes down the stairs.

At the front door he runs into Hug with his finger on the buzzer. His only greeting is what's up with the paintings and doesn't he realize that they've already sold them all, the day before yesterday already, even before they were done. He calls him to task, if nothing more than because half the planet is already involved. The buyers have already been selected, as well as the museums that will aquire some of the works. He complains, in passing, about how Helena does things and reminds him of the good old days when

Hug was calling the shots. He announces that the titles of the paintings (for which they have commissioned an advertising copywriter) have already been chosen. They are vague enough to adapt to whatever he paints, no matter what it is. He supposed that Heribert won't mind, since putting names to his paintings is a job he's not fond of, and reminds him that when they met all his paintings bore the same title: *Untitled*. He informs him that they have managed to place a painting with Peter Ludwig, who has called from Germany to learn when the exhibition will be closing and, hence, the exact date on which they will be sending the painting. Morton Neumann is in from Chicago to talk with Helena. He reminds him that the opening is the twenty-second, so he should do it however he can. He reminds him how hard it has been to get this far. He asks him if what he wants is for Hug to paint them himself, or if he's trying to be cool or play the *enfant terrible*. Lowering his voice, he observes that at this stage of the century, playing the *enfant terrible* is not the recipe for success it once was. Or is it?

Heribert feels revulsion for a person so full of doubts. He leaps to one side, stops a cab, swings the door open, and, to keep Hug out, gives him a good kick in the shins.

He gets out in front of a stamp shop. He looks one by one at the hundreds of orderly stamps in the window. They seem boring, and if it weren't for their considerable price, he would have categorized them along with trading cards in terms of the interest they awakened in him. Some of them show drawings of old airplanes, some extremely strange birds, some very serious faces, generals with wigs, horrible flowers. Some, just a few, have been cancelled. What *real* purpose do they serve, then, if they are no longer good for mailing letters? Maybe what he needs to do is to begin collecting them even though he's not into it—with time and habit, he'll get into it eventually. He opens the door to the store. They greet him with excessive cordiality. The counter is made of glass, and underneath there are row and rows of stamps. He looks at a very strange series (it seems very strange to him) with drawings of very strange fish, from a country with a very strange name, which he doesn't even recognize from having studied it at school. He asks the price.

"Seven hundred dollars."

"I'll take it."

"Seven hundred dollars each, sir, not the series."

"How many are there in the series?"

"Twenty."

"Do you accept checks, or credit cards?"

"Visa and MasterCard, sir. Checks only if . . ."

"I'll take them, then. Show me a few more series; interesting, hard-to-find ones . . ."

He leaves with thirty-eight complete series and hundreds of loose stamps. There is a Cuban stamp, with a military officer sporting a bushy mustache and long white sideburns, which he finds particularly appealing, despite the fact that, according to the information they have provided at the store, it is of slight value. He has taken all the stamps from Gabon, Lesotho, Cameroon, Mongolia, Hungary, Rwanda, Zaire, Bhutan, France, Andorra, Brazil, Mexico, Paraguay, Nicaragua, Romania, Malta, New Caledonia, Libya, Czechoslovakia, Mozambique, Tonga, Benin, Mali, the Dominican Republic, and Wallis and Futuna. And Turks and Caicos, with images of football players facing off over a ball. He takes stamps with images of birds: from Christmas Island and the Seychelles, from Bhutan, from Aitutaki, from the Solomon Islands, from Vanuatu Vatu, from Botswana, from Tanzania, from Swaziland, from Portugal, from Norway, from East Germany, from Monaco, from the Netherlands, from Yugoslavia, from the Bahamas, from Barbados, and from the British Virgin Islands. He takes some with images of flowers: from Vanuatu Vatu, from Hungary, from Sri Lanka, from Wallis and Futuna, from India, from Afghanistan, from Laos, from Italy, from Bulgaria, from the Solomon Islands, from China, from Montserrat, from Argentina, from Rwanda, from Ghana, from Mali, from Niue, from Oman, from Ireland. He takes some from Pakistan (with images of the blind dolphin of the Indus River), from Jamaica (with sea cows). He takes some with whale figures: from Australia and Norfolk Island. From the Unites States he takes images of Jackie Robinson, of Harriet Tubman, of Martin Luther King, of Benjamin Banneker, of Whitney Moore Young: the complete Black Heritage series. He also takes some commemorative stamps from the twenty-first birthday celebration of the Princess of Wales: from the Ascension Islands, from the Bahamas, from Barbados, from the British Antarctic Territory, from the Cayman Islands, from the Falkland Islands, from the Fiji Islands, from Gambia, from Mauritius, from Pitcairn Island, from Santa Helena Island, from the Solomon Islands, from Swaziland, from Tristan da Cunha, from Antigua and Barbuda, from Cameroon, from Ghana, from Togo, from Bhutan, from Dominica, from Grenada, from the Maldive Islands, from Sierra Leone, from the Turks and Caicos Islands, from Uganda, from Anguilla. He also bought stamps of Princess Catherine of Aragon, of Anne Neville, of Caroline of Brandenburg-Ansbach, of Augusta of Saxe-Gotha, of Caroline of Brunswick, Alexandra of Denmark, and of Queen Mary (the wife of George V of England), emitted by Tuvalu, Montserrat, Saint Vincent, Saint Kitts and Nevis, and Kiribati. On a shelf there is an engraving of a philatelist contemplating his collection, with a magnifying glass in the left hand and tongs in the right. So he also requests a magnifying glass and tongs. He pays, they put it all in a couple of bags, and he goes out into the street. He stops a cab. He gets in. He unfolds the yellow pages he tore out of the telephone book. He reads out another address. The taxi takes off. He folds the sheets and puts them back in his pocket. The taxi drops him at a numismatist's.

No sooner has he entered then he asks, in a loud voice, if they have Roman coins. He feels like a tourist in a strange land, proudly ordering paella with chocolate milk. He asks to see Roman coins because they seem like the biggest cliché in coin collecting.

They advise against Roman coins, because at present they are not a good investment. He could have asked for Greek coins, though. Or Egyptian ones. Was there any such thing as Egyptian coins?

"It doesn't matter. I'll take Roman coins, if you have any. Do they come in series, like stamps?"

The woman is dumbfounded.

"Bring them out, bring them out. Did the Egyptians have coins?"

He leaves under the weight of two more bags, full of coins: Roman, Greek, medieval, modern . . . He had a continental dollar coin from 1776, made of pewter; an Augustus Humbert from 1851, a silver dollar from 1779, which had never been in circulation; two quarters from 1829, also never placed in circulation; a double eagle from 1886, which had hardly circulated; an eagle quarter from 1834, never circulated; two half eagles from 1829, never circulated; a double eagle from 1886, hardly circulated; a quarter eagle from 1834, never circulated; two half eagles from 1829, never circulated; a set of five gold pieces from 1866; a 1913-S Barber quarter, never circulated; a fifty-dollar Panama-Pacific commemorative gold coin, never circulated; a Peace dollar proof from 1921; many 1949-S Franklin half dollars with full bell lines; Standing Liberty quarters with full head; German medallions from the Hindenburg and Hitler period; medals from Panama and the Panama Canal; medals from William Penn and Pennsylvania; a complete set of Stellas; 1860-D and 1875 gold dollars; 1797, 1854-S, and 1875 eagle quarters; half eagles from 1827 and 1887; 100 ducat gold pieces from Ferdinand III, Archduke of Austria, dated 1629; several 1870-CC double eagles; 1794 large cents; an 1819 half eagle; an 1849 ten-dollar piece from the Cincinnati Mining & Trading Co.; Kennedy half-dollars; Susan B. Anthony dollars; and one five-shilling proof piece from Charles II of England, 1662 . . . But he's not satisfied. He wants Egyptian coins, Asian ones . . . He takes a cab. When the driver asks where he wants to go, Heribert asks himself why he got into a cab, and so as not to tell the driver that he doesn't want to anywhere, he says to the corner. He pays the minuscule fare and tips him with a five-shilling piece from 1662 with the face of Charles III of England. He walks through the theater district; it's full of couples dressed to the nines, in tuxedos and long gowns, with shining eyes. The corners are full of musicians, magicians doing tricks, and jugglers. In each of their hats he deposits coins of the Caesars, maravedis, Brazilian coins from the time of the Pedro the Emperor, rubles with the faces of the czars. He doesn't see the point, though, in numismatism. What was it that moved people to collect things? On the corner, close to a police car with spinning lights, he sees a man stretched out on the ground. His eyeglasses lie a yard away, in pieces. There is a slit in his head from which a great deal of blood has flowed, leaving a stain on the ground. The bicycle, not far away, is as twisted as one an acrobat was using not long before. If only he felt something . . . He vows to leave the door unlocked when he gets home. If someone assaulted him, if someone robbed his apartment, if someone wounded him, if he had an accident, if he were murdered . . . Why was it always someone else who was robbed, wounded, or murdered? This question seems too tragic, though, and he keeps walking as he imagines that if the cyclist had fallen in the snow instead of on the asphalt, the red stain would have gained by contrast.

•

Humbert sits exactly where Heribert tells him too. His docility leads Heribert to think that he has sat in the precise spot where the imaginary line stretching from his index finger to the sofa ends. He thinks that if he had told him to sit on the floor or jump out the window, he would also have done that. Or is it that he had imagined him so conceited that now, in contrast, he seems humble, overly humble? The collections of stamps and coins sit on the table. As Humbert rattles on, Heribert wonders if it would be appropriate to ask him if he likes collecting things, if he had ever collected stamps and, if he had, why; if, as a child, he had collected coins or trading cards or, as an adult, movie listings, match boxes, key chains, pencils, exotic cigarette packages, palindromic train or tram tickets. Oh, how he loves palindromes! He would have asked if collecting things made him feel anything special, if it was exciting, if he knows what other people who collected things felt about it. In the meantime, Humbert is asking him for advice about opportunities for exhibitions, about the possibility that he might, *in some way*, take him under his wing. He asks him to stop by the studio where he lives and works, to see his paintings. Heribert vaguely says yes to everything, trying not to listen too hard to what he's saying. As for taking him under his wing, Humbert says, Helena (who has seen his paintings and has found them very interesting) thinks that if he (Heribert Julià) were to offer the slightest gesture of support, then he (Humbert Herrera) could get off to a good start, a, shall we say, respectable start, in this shady art world . . .

Heribert looks closely at him: green glasses! He has seen those green glasses, and the face behind them, not very long before, somewhere, and not just once. As soon as he remembers where, he is surprised at having taken so long to recognize him: this is the man who is seeing Helena! He is astonished. He smiles. Pleasantly astonished, because, in some way, to have discovered him and have him right there must give him a certain advantage. Over what? What kind of advantage? Why? He is suddenly very interested in seeing Humbert's paintings. Right away.

They have long since fallen into an uncomfortable silence, which Humbert can't seem to break, and which Heribert is unaware of because he is trying to think, and thinking requires a great deal of concentration. When he finally notices, he tries to correct the bad impression and smiles again.

"Can we go see your paintings now?" he asks, quite sincerely.

"Now? The light is terrible . . . It would be better in daylight."

Heribert looks out the window. The sky is dark. If, before seeing the sky, someone had asked him what time of day it was, or even if it were day or night, he wouldn't have known what to say. He then tries to deduce whether it is early evening or already well into the night. He seems to remember that he has arranged to see Herundina this evening. When he searches his memory, he even recalls the time and place. He couldn't say whether he was pleased or not at having remembered.

"Tomorrow would be better," says Humbert, "if that's all right . . ."

"Sure. In any case, I have to catch up with a girl for dinner now," he says, smiling the whole time, all the while thinking that he is smiling and saying this to put the young man at ease, letting him know that (in the event he ever finds out that Heribert knows he is Helena's lover) he shouldn't worry, as the fact that he is going to bed with her not only doesn't bother him but is (and this is the proof) the only thing that could have made him take an interest in him.

He shows him to the door. When he says goodbye, he shakes his hand effusively, taking it between both of his own, and is on the verge of giving him a kiss on the forehead. He gathers up the coins and the stamps, puts them in plastic bags, and leaves them in the closet where (the day before? that same day? a week ago?) he stored the wig, the heart-shaped glasses, the plastic ball, and the flowered pants. As he takes his jacket off the hanger and goes outside, he wonders if he has made a good impression on Humbert.

He has dinner with Herundina in a quiet restaurant, where everyone speaks softly amid white tablecloths in an overheated roof garden with ivy-covered brick walls. The table they are sitting at is a bit wobbly. They ought to prop it up, but since they don't, Heribert spends the whole time making it wobble. They order chocolate mousse for dessert. Heribert paints a mustache on his face with it. When Herundina laughs, Heribert glares at her and bangs his fist on the table. The other diners turn their heads to look at them. Herundina, half amazed, half frightened, blushes in embarrassment, on the verge of tears.

"You're very strange."

"You said that the other day. Repeating oneself is a symptom of death . . ."

A half hour later they are one their way out of the city in Herundina's car. Heribert hasn't driven in a while, and when he steps on the accelerator everything around him accelerates. But he looks at the speedometer and he's not speeding. What's more, if he speeds up noticeably, the girl will surely protest. For a moment, he closes his eyes, and he feels a landslide, the propeller of a small plane gathering speed, an intermittent whistling that grows louder and louder. When he opens his eyes, the highway is still in place. He closes them again. He counts to five seconds. He opens them. Everything in order. He closes his eyes again. He counts to ten seconds. He opens them. There's a van a short distance ahead. He accelerates and leaves it behind. He closes his eyes again. He counts to ten seconds and doesn't open them. He counts to fifteen in all. He imagines the sound of the car crashing into a truck and being crushed, of being crushed himself.

When he opens his eyes, though, he isn't even close to the ditch. They have left the city behind, and on either side of the road there is nothing but one-story homes and cemeteries, and an occasional empty lot.

After about forty-five minutes, they see a hotel close to the road, half-hidden between the trees, the lights on the ground floor lit. They turn onto the gravel path that leads to it. They park out in front. Heribert hastens to open the door on the young woman's side.

It is a little wooden hotel painted white with tables set up on the verandah. On each table a red candle is burning. Heribert finds it strange that they have set up tables outside in that cold. Herundina declares that she is about to freeze. Heribert sits down anyway. Herundina does, too; her breath forms clouds. The door creaks. A kindly old man comes out to serve them. They order a bottle of champagne. He brings it out, with two glasses. Herundina says once again that she's cold. The man tells them they can go inside. Heribert says it doesn't matter. Herundina looks at him, taken aback. The man struggles to uncork the bottle, and just before he does, they hear his spine crack. They down the champagne, and it goes right to their heads. Herundina laughs and tilts back and forth on the legs of her chair. An old woman spies on them from the window, drawing the curtain back with a bony head. When Herundina says the champagne has warmed her up, Heribert gets up and suggests going inside. The old woman moves away from the window. The proprietor is running a dishcloth along the countertop. The room is empty.

They order another bottle. He brings it over. As he opens it, Heribert asks if they have any rooms available. He says it suddenly, without thinking, and once he's said it he thinks it's an excellent idea. He decides that if Herundina makes a fuss or looks outraged, he will smack her. But Herundina smiles, gazing at him with enormous eyes. The old man tells them that at this time of year the hotel is never full, though in the summer it's another story since they're right on the beach.

"All the other hotels (as you must already have noticed) are closed. There's no business in it. We only open because if we didn't, what would we do? Our children are all grown, they live in the city, and if we stay open, someone always happens along, like you folks . . ."

He gives them the key. They go up to the room with the bottle and the glasses. From the window you can see an endless stretch of woods, blacker even than the sky above it, and to the left, points of light. They must be houses. The place is silent, but the floorboards creak. Heribert fills both glasses with champagne and locks the door from inside. Herundina embraces him. Heribert would have been irritated if Herundina hadn't wanted to come upstairs, but now that they're there he feels rather annoyed by the embrace. Too weary to come up with a convincing excuse, he indolently lets her proceed.

•

The heat is up so high that Heribert is sweating and the sheets are sticking to his skin. The sound of a television reaches him from the ground floor. The couple must be watching TV. Heribert glances at the clock. It's 1:00 A.M. What should he do now? Go right home? Wait for her to wake up? He could grab the cars keys, take off, and leave her there, fast asleep.

At 1:30 he looks at the young woman's broad back. At 1:57, her slender waist. At 2:07, the shadowy crack between the cheeks of her ass. At 2:30, the whiter triangle that (he thinks at 2:45) must be the negative of the panties she wears when she tans herself under infrared lights or in the snow (he thinks at three o'clock). At 3:45 he thinks that, in fact, all he had felt for Herundina was desire.

It had taken him hours to formulate this thought. When Herundina wakes up, it's 4:00 A.M. She sees Heribert looking at her. She smiles at him. He isn't sure whether or not to smile back. She puts her arms around him, and brings her mouth close to his.

One hour later, the old couple waves goodbye from the verandah. Heribert and Herundina take the road back to the city. Herundina wants to go with him to see the two paintings he's had at the Whitney for a few months now.

They leave the car in a nearby parking lot. They walk arm in arm through the first few galleries. Herundina asks him if he's been a citizen for long. He says for twelve years. She asks how long he's lived here. He says since he was four years old. They go up to the second floor. Before two adjoining rooms, Herundina pulls in one direction and Heribert in the other. As he pulls Herundina, without really knowing why, toward the room she doesn't want to go into, Heribert feels that the building reminds him of the cemeteries he had seen from the car the night before.

"You're not very nice. Why don't you want to come see your paintings with me now?"

Eyes closed, as if blind, he accompanies her till she comes to a halt. Then he opens his eyes and finds himself before two walls at an angle. There are two canvases; he finds it hard to identify them as his. When Heribert hears the girl say she's in love with him, no matter how obtuse, stubborn, and distant he wants to appear, a chill runs up his spine. Feeling lost, he goes over to the corner formed by the two walls and rests against it. What should he say to her? He can tell her that there was a time when he liked her, that, at times, when he was in bed caressing her sister, he would pretend he was caressing her. When he looks up, a figure too dark and mustachioed to be Herundina is standing before him. "Good thing I didn't think of hugging her with my eyes closed," he thinks.

Herundina watches as the gallery guard reprimands Heribert. As he apologizes, Heribert considers the thought of lying and telling Herundina he loves her. Where would that lead, though? If he had never lied, he could resolve to commence a new life, always lying without fail, firmly vowing never again to utter so much as a single truth. Even if it were completely false, he would make the woman very happy if he declared his love for her, and in point of fact, it wouldn't be all that hard. That must be the solution. There can't possibly be another. They leave the gallery. They walk through the museum without looking at a single painting. Heribert opens his mouth and says, very slowly:

"I love you."

Herundina's expression wavers between happiness and stupefaction. Is she not sure whether or not to believe him? All he needed now was for her not to believe him, after the effort he's put into saying it. Her draws her close to him, takes her in his arms, and kisses her. Kissing is so easy, even if you don't feel like it. As he kisses her, he sees a girl, who looks vaguely familiar, walk by *The Paris Bit* by Stuart Davis. "She looks like an Anna, or an Anne . . ." He remembers: she was the girl from a few days ago at the bookstore, the one he had involuntarily kept from stealing a book! It would be so easy for him to feel desire for her . . . It would be so easy, later on, to stop feeling desire for her . . . At that very moment he is feeling it, desire, a faint desire that (if he keeps looking at her much longer) will grow increasingly strong (or weak, or even disappear if he turns his head and looks at one of those paintings, or at the floor, or at the ceiling, and forgets her). What if everything were different with her, though? Maybe he will only be able to grab onto something when he no longer expects anything. He watches the girl vanish into another gallery. He makes a move to follow her.

"Answer me. Do you want to or not? Hey . . . you weren't listening!"

He looks at the woman in his arms and steps back. He recalls her name, but can no longer form a single thought about her. She extricates herself from his embrace; furious, she strikes him and flees down the stairs. Heribert bursts out laughing, runs his hand over his stinging cheek, and thinks maybe he should follow her, tell her he was sorry, that he had been listening to her, or that he hadn't, that all he heard was the mellifluous flow of her marvelously harmonious voice, as if it were music: that was how much in love he was. She would never buy it, though. Or would she? (And what about mellifluous? What exactly did it mean?) For a moment, the urge to know whether or not she would go for that story has him on the verge of dashing down the stairs after her. Instead, he heads toward the adjoining room. The girl from the bookstore isn't there. He looks in all the other galleries until he sees her in front of *The Brass Family*, by Alexander Calder. Heribert positions himself by her side, slowly turns his head, and looks at her. The girl also turns her head and looks at him. Heribert feels an intense attraction to her, and he is certain she feels the same for him, so certain he feels they need not so much as say a word to understand what they feel for each other. Finally, there is someone with whom words will be superfluous, and perhaps nothing he has experienced till now would make any sense were it not for this encounter, which in contrast now gives meaning to everything. He moves close to her and smiles.

•

He caresses her thigh; he kisses her on the neck. She opens her mouth; she kisses his tongue. They were in a museum hallway, near the telephone booths. She suggests they go for coffee.

They sit at a table. They order coffee. The waiter brings it. The girl pays for it. She says she's delighted to buy coffee for such a prestigious artist. He picks up the cup and pours the coffee over his head. She laughs and asks him again if he hasn't been drinking. Heribert says no, and to prove it, he gets up from the chair and balances himself on his left foot while raising his right thigh until it is parallel to the ground. Then he places the thumb of his right hand at the tip of his nose while simultaneously stretching his palm and inclining his trunk until he almost touches his knee with the pinky of the same hand. Having stood like that for ten seconds without losing his balance, he salutes the girl and the customers in the cafeteria, who were staring at him, and sits back down. The girl laughs.

"Not drunk. You're just crazy."

They embrace again. Heribert puts his hand under her skirt, and when she protests, he stays still. But when she can no longer stifle her laughter, finally bursting out, Heribert tries to caress her pubis. The young woman finishes her coffee, they get up from the table, and begin to run after each other from room to room, going up and down the museum stairs and playing a combination of tag and hide-and-seek. At last, exhausted, they rest against *Standing Woman* by Gaston Lachaise. Little by little they slide down until they are sitting on the floor. They are caught in such a feverish embrace that when Heribert notices that the sculpture is moving he thinks for a moment that passion can make even the most immutable works kinetic. When he lifts his head, he barely has time to register that the guard's gestures are not reprimands and the astonishment on the museum visitors' faces is not censure, before, a tenth of a second later, he feels all the bronze of that larger-than-life and generously-proportioned woman crashing down on him and begins to understand what is really happening.

•

When he opens his eyes he doesn't know what day it is, or what time, or how many days, hours, and minutes have gone by since the last time he opened his eyes, nor how many more will go by from the moment in which he closes them again.

•

Sunlight streams in through the window and lights up the wall at the foot of the bed. The first thing he sees is the flower arrangement. Then he looks down at his body, vaguely convinced it will be shorter than it was before. One of his legs, the right one, is in a cast. And one arm, also the right.

He feels comfortable in that bed. He turns his head. To one side there is a night table with water, bottles, and small objects whose functions are unknown to him. His whole body hurts. He looks up. He sees a small panel with buttons. One of them shows an outline of a light bulb with rays of light. The other shows a female silhouette with a skirt, a cap, and a line in her hand; it must represent a tray. He concludes that this is the button to call the nurse. He presses it. A half a minute later a young woman appears. "What if I can't speak?" he thinks. Perhaps as a result of the accident he won't be able to articulate a single sound. He's afraid to put it to the test and discover it's true. What if his tongue has been cut off? Or if he severed it himself, on impact? Impact . . . He imagines his tongue on the ground, like a lizard's tail. With a life of its own. And what about his face? Maybe his face is deformed. Maybe a terrifying scar has turned him into a monster. The nurse looks at him understandingly and tells him a slew of things. So he can hear, then; he's pleased. He makes an effort to understand what the woman is saying. She is saying soothing things. She's speaking to him as if he were retarded. Maybe the blow has turned him into an idiot. But an idiot wouldn't think such a thing. Or would he? Maybe he has been an idiot all his life and the blow brought him to his senses. He opens his mouth and manages to utter one word, then two, then three: a whole sentence. He can talk, too. He closes first one eye, then the other. He has two, then. He asks for a mirror and details about his condition. The woman says he has broken an arm and a leg, and that the museum administration is astonished that such a thing could have happened. Technically it was quite impossible for the sculpture to fall. Heribert doesn't find it so strange: everything is impossible until it happens, above all such bizarre events as this.

What if he can never paint again? Perhaps he is crippled, or will be an invalid for life. He requests a diagnosis. The nurse doesn't know. He will have to ask the doctor. Maybe that's what he needs, something to grab onto: the struggle to overcome an infirmity. He asks what day it is. Friday the 8th. He was admitted the day before. He's only been there for one day?

If she had said it was a month he would have believed it all the same. He can still decide, sick as he is, to make a heroic gesture and do the paintings for the exhibition: a feat worthy of a Greek demigod.

·

Helena arrives with a bouquet of flowers. Heribert recalls that just a short time before he had seen another bouquet of flowers. He looks around the room and quickly locates it, in a corner. Someone must have moved it. What a coincidence: two bouquets of flowers. Life is full of coincidences. One bouquet and another bouquet are a coincidence. He tries to find more. Helena has two feet, and so does he: voilà, another coincidence. He looks for more. A window with a blind and, next to it, another window with a blind: another coincidence. Looking for more is harder for him. He thinks that he has come up with quite enough for the first try: no need to overdo it.

"Who brought the other bouquet?"

"Humbert. You remember him, don't you?"

·

The doctor seems like a good man. He jokes with him the whole time. He asks what the paintings he does from now on will be worth in the event they can't save his leg and they have to amputate it, or if one arm ends up a bit shorter than the other? Will they be worth more or less than the ones he had done before? He also tells him not to mess with the nurses, and he smiles to show that it is only a joke. Heribert finds him charming and intelligent and makes a firm pledge to speak with him at length, some day.

·

There is a knock at the door. Heribert says to come in. Hug comes roaring into the room, telling him that Helena has decided to put on the exhibition any way she can, that they are all casting about for an idea that can save them. Heribert closes his eyes, hides his head under the pillow, and when Hug doesn't leave, he calls for the nurse and asks her to escort him out.

·

The doctor's comments lead him to think he has not devoted much attention to the nurses, which he proceeds to do from that moment on. The nurse on the night shift is more attractive than the one on the day shift. Maybe now that he's all banged up he'll start feeling passionate again. What's more, nurses have always been a persistent part of popular erotic mythology, leading one to foresee miracles. At one point, when the night nurse is picking things up from the bedside table, Heribert lifts his hand to caress her thigh, but then lowers it. He concentrates on counting the tiles, the bars on the bed . . . He could add them all together . . . but what a bore! If here were in a ward, with a lot of other patients, he could watch them, make fun of them, listen to their conversations. He would have company. But no sooner does he have this thought than he realizes it would be horrible to have to put up with all that half-dead, skinny, pale, sick riffraff and their crying and moaning. Let them all die! He doesn't want to see them! How glad he is to be in a room by himself!

·

He reads an article in the newspaper about the creative crises many painters, filmmakers, and musicians are going through nowadays. "Is there anything left to say?" the journalist asks. "Lately, the speed with which new fashions and cultural tastes succeed each other leads one . . ." He drops the paper. He picks up a novel Hilari has lent him, in which there are no dead bodies. He used to think they were boring. Now he thinks the ones with dead bodies are phony.

·

The doctor comes in, with traces of blood on his gown and in need of a shave. There is a nurse with him. They are standing by the side of the bed, looking at him with a smile Heribert finds hard to categorize. The doctor announces that they will be releasing him that evening. He is much better. Soon, the doctor says, if he puts his mind to it he will be able to paint again. Heribert's blood boils. What is this fool saying? How dare he insinuate something like that? What does he know about it? He had thought him to be an intelligent man, and now he comes out with this nonsense! He musters all the strength he has and spits at him. The arc of the sputum is weaker than he had intended, and it falls on the sheet on top of him. The expression on the doctor's face changes and gets serious. The nurse wipes the spittle off with a Kleenex. There is a knock at the door. Helena comes in. She speaks with the doctor. Heribert studies the two of them, one right next to the other: Helena and the doctor, observing him. "Is she also getting it on with this quack?" Then the doctor and nurse leave the room. Helena has brought another bouquet of flowers. Why so many flowers? Heribert tries to think of some vulgar phrase that will annoy her, like: "Bring me a nice little eleven-year-old girl, and don't bring me any more flowers," but it seems like a cheap shot. For some time now (ever since the doctor and nurse had left), Helena has been telling him that the following day there will be a business lunch at their house, and that Hug will be there, along with other people who have money in the gallery, and Humbert. They have to fill the gap he has left them in, and they can't do it just any old way. There were just a few days left, and they had to find an artist whose work was so good that this deplorable incident would not have lasting consequences for the gallery. They have to create a brilliant success, turn this error into a new leap forward, convert a debit into an asset. They have to use this opening to fly higher. This is why they can't use a vaguely-familiar, second-rate artist—it would be like admitting defeat. There is only one possible move: they must introduce a complete unknown, someone whose body of work would amaze the critics, the public, and collectors alike. Humbert has the stuff. Tomorrow, all of them, together, will discuss what has to be done, and she's telling him now so that he doesn't think they've been plotting behind his back. But Heribert has been thinking the whole time about the "leap forward." About how perfect metaphors, and strings of metaphors, were for whiling away the hours at play. Why can't he just stay forevermore in that place, where, as if by a secret pact, everything is white and everyone is dressed in white, juggling similes and metaphors like a circus performer?

DECEMBER

"Where to, kid?"

"Where?"

"Yes, where. What else?"

"Oh, I thought you meant it figuratively."

—Francesc Trabal, *L'any que ve*

He is dreaming of a swimming pool like the one he is sitting beside: white, spotless, blurred as if drawn in pencil and watercolors; or like a Hockney: lots of colorful awnings and tables with tall glasses. A woman with dark glasses is lying in a white hammock, sunbathing. It's Helena. When she realizes he's watching her, she smiles, raises her sunglasses until they are resting on the top of her head, looks back at him, and opens her mouth as if she were speaking, without emitting any sound. And, even though her voice can't be heard, she is saying: "I'm upset you don't want to make love with me." "Make love!" Humbert snorts, and dives into the pool, where everything is warm and light blue, and he can swim for ages and ages underwater without having to come up to the surface for air. It was so easy to breathe underwater . . . You just had to open your mouth like a fish out of water, but unlike a suffocating fish (for whom air is a foreign medium), he can breathe perfectly. "What a shame," he thinks, "that this pool is only a drawing, so the sounds from above can't reach me. Though sound wouldn't reach me in a real pool, either." When his head comes to the surface, Helena, who is sitting on the edge of the pool and splashing her feet in the water, is looking at him from behind her dark glasses, set against a desert background filled with singing Berbers. She has a straw sun hat on. "Do you love me?" she asks. In response, Humbert simply bites her foot, and everything goes into slow motion. Helena says, "Sometimes I think you've never loved me, and I mean nothing more to you than that diving board." "What a great image," Humbert thinks, "the diving board. As if it had all these different registers and levels of meaning . . ." He hears someone laugh. He looks at the diving board, but the sun hurts his eyes, and he is now back in the water, his lungs full of air. He contemplates the bubbles that come out of his mouth. He thinks, "When I get out now, there'll be a beer by the side of the pool." When he gets out, a smiling Helena hands him an icy mug of beer with a snow-white head which drips and falls into the water, leaving patches of color that shouldn't . . . As he drinks the mug down, Helena kisses him on the forehead. "If only it could always be like this . . ." He plunges back into the water and thinks, "When I get out, I want this house surrounding us, the house I live in, to be gone. I want to be on a beach." He gets out and opens his eyes: he is on a beach. Wincing at the sunlight, he goes under again. "When I get out, I want to see the signature of the Hockney I'm in, in a corner somewhere." When he gets out, in a corner of the sky (a cardboard sky right over his head) he sees Hockney's signature, fading away as if written in smoke. Every time he gets out the sun pierces his eyes. If only he could always live under water . . . "I could live there forever if it weren't for the fact that every time I come up the sunlight hurts my eyes, and the longer and longer I stay under, and the longer and longer I take to come out again, the more it will hurt, until the times comes when I will bleed like a Christ figure, like a menstruating woman, like a wounded soldier, like a fish in a basket . . ." A man jumps out a window and falls onto a tumbling mat. He runs down the street. Death is so sad. If he could only hide in a shadow . . . To hide in a shadow is like not being there at all; he can only be touched or nabbed if he is in the sun, but then he has to stop, surrounded by the sands of a desert in the center of the world, under a red sun wearing dark glasses with frames the color of the girls riding down the highway on bicycles, on their way home, never arriving because they get lost on dirt trails, beyond the fences, rolling up the mountainside, those girls in the pictures of Helena as a teenager, sitting in meadows, wearing short skirts and high-heeled shoes, always smiling, wearing short pants and socks, with those flaming lips that scorch you as you die with pleasure.

·

Humbert wakes up when the rays of sunlight hit his face with such intensity that it hurts. He opens his eyes, looks at his watch (1:30), and jumps out of the lawn chair. He does some push-ups. He thinks, "I wouldn't mind having an orange juice now." He leans on the porch rail and looks toward the pool. "I would love to paint a pool. If only it hadn't been done so often . . ." He puts on shorts and thin-soled shoes. He goes toward the kitchen. He peels an orange. He eats it. He takes out four more, turns on the squeezer, and prepares himself an orange juice.

In the bungalow where he has his studio, he sits down at the table. Against the long wall rests a row of eight half-painted canvases. He gathers up the newspaper clippings, organizes them, and he reads snatches from them as he files them in different folders. The *Times* says, "Rarely in the history of contemporary art has there been a more meteoric rise than that of Humbert Herrera. We have certainly become accustomed, of late, to more or less rapid ascensions—a case in point being that of Heribert Julià, whose unfortunate accident is responsible for our making the acquaintance of Herrera, who, as Julià's replacement, has produced his first, and definitive, exhibition . . ." *La Reppublica* says: "With the exception of Miró, the most renowned Catalan artist to precede Julià and Herrera, perhaps not since Picasso's death has an artist so exclusively captured the attention . . ." Another, from *O Globo*: "After two solid decades of artistic disarray, of wave upon wave of pictorial fads, each superimposed one upon the other, finally one young man—and his youth must be stressed, for it holds out great hope for the art world—seems at last to have taken up the challenge of art as a totality, and has responded with a cohesive body of work which—though written off as a hodge-podge by envious pens—manages to make eclectic and unselfconscious use of elements taken from all the artistic trends of these years of confusion, from conceptualism to the new expressionism, to build an articulated body of work—perhaps the most coherent oeuvre of the post-modern aesthetic. Herrera plays all the chords of human sentiment and ratiocination, from tenderness to irony, to cynicism, thus taking up where the extraordinary momentum of Heribert Julià's appearance little more than a year ago left off. Needless to say, the art world hopes that this new direction will be consolidated and not turn out to be, as has occurred on so many recent occasions, a mere promise, frustrated in the end . . ."

He looks through his mail. A postcard from Tokyo: "Even before opening, almost everything is already sold. Ciao, Xano." A package: the finished catalog for the Milan exhibition. He closes his eyes to daydream. He'd like to celebrate the opening of the exhibition by turning off all the lights in Milan for one night; the only lights on would be those of the gallery. On a white sheet of paper filled with notes he writes: "Speak with Milan City Hall." And when they ask why? Humbert observes that the lack of a theoretical framework, common to all the latest generation of painters, while handy on occasions, is problematic at other times. He takes a notebook from the desk drawer and writes: "Smooth out the rough edges of the theoretical framework, particularly with regard to alterations in the routines of big cities." Another postcard from Xano, dated two days after the previous one: "Paintings not sold before opening are now sold. Keep up the good work! Big hug, Xano." A letter from an Australian museum requesting more paintings. He thinks: "Odd that I don't have any in New Zealand yet." On the sheet full of notes he writes: "Find out what's going on with New Zealand." He takes another notebook out of the drawer with the word PAINTINGS on the cover and jots down: "Do a totally disconcerting and false landscape and title it *New Zealand*."

He feels happy. There's so much to do! The notebook labeled PAINTINGS is full of notes. "So many paintings I'll never get to . . . Life is too short for all the work one could do. I ought to hire people, find a team of collaborators to assist me." He takes out a notebook, the one where he wrote about smoothing out the theoretical framework—labeled IDEAS—and writes: "Find team of collaborators. Or commission paintings to others? Commission other artists to paint them? Would they be offended? How about selling them the ideas so that they can develop them, or use them as is?" He shuts the notebook and drops it on top of another one that says ENVIRONMENTS.

Helena is turning the gold doorknob on the bungalow door. Humbert jumps up from his chair and goes over to hug her. They kiss. Helena carefully spreads the contents of the bag she is carrying on the floor: cheeses, pâtés, spinach salad and cole slaw, apples, frozen yogurt, and a bottle of vodka. Humbert looks at the label, takes the PAINTINGS notebook out of the drawer, and writes: "Do fake labels." Then he thinks better of it: he crosses it out, puts the book in the drawer, and takes out another one, labeled OBJECTS. He writes: "Do fake wine labels, fake jars, fake wrappings. Do cardboard boxes for liquid products: soup, wine . . . Do plastic bottles with fine wine labels. Do tin cans for champagne."

"I'm starved . . ." Humbert says.

They eat the cheese, the pâtés, the salad and slaw, the apples, and the frozen yogurt. They open the vodka, drink from the bottle, and have sex on the floor. When they are finished, Humbert gets up, opens the PAINTINGS notebook, and writes: "Couples having sex, in many colors and extravagant positions." He thinks for a moment and adds another line: "Totally black painting titled *Love in the Dark*." In the ENVIRONMENTS book he writes: "A boxing ring completely covered over with a white sheet. Audience in bleachers. In the ring boxers fight unseen by audience." He opens another notebook, labeled CONCEPTS, and writes: "A dictionary with all the 'obscene' entries crossed out and replaced with 'proper' entries. And vice-versa. Two dictionaries, then. Possible variations: rewriting of political, urbanistic, botanical, and psychological terminologies . . ." He shuts the notebook and looks at it. Though Helena didn't see eye to eye with him at all on this, and thought that he would be better off tossing notebooks titled CONCEPTS and ENVIRONMENTS into the fire, he believes that those, shall we say, "objectual" styles of the previous decade, done with a little bit of flair, would not have passed under the art-business radar without a trace.

"Don't you think conceptualism would have been more fruitful if it had been done with a little more style and wit?"

Helena doesn't answer. She's fast asleep. He looks closely at her, stretched out face down on the floor of the studio, amid the salad bowls and wine glasses. Two men burst through the door and, just as she is lying, face down, they use her sexually (use her sexually?), like animals. Not two men, three. He takes out the PAINTINGS notebook and jots down: "Variation on the theme of the painter and his model, as done above all by Picasso: the model with two or three men, and the painter watching and painting, or with a video camera." He takes out the VIDEOS notebook and "Reflect on pornography in video." Then he does a couple of sketches of Helena in soft pencil on sheets of paper. He also takes out his camera and photographs her. He takes advantage of the time she is asleep to finish up three of the half-finished paintings, plan five new ones, and read a brief guide to Jamaican art that he had picked up at the airport when they landed. When Helena wakes up they have sex again, and afterwards he dashes right down to the swimming pool and dives in.

He puts on a pair of shorts and a Hawaiian shirt. He combs his hair in front of the mirror. He walks slowly down the steps. The reporter is waiting for him next to the pool. He is disappointed that he is not wearing a fedora with a PRESS card sticking out of the hatband. His showing up in that Texan shirt, those dark glasses, and that can-do attitude were all annoying details that denoted a certain disregard. The reporter gets up from the lawn chair he's been sitting on, comes over with his hand stretched out, and thanks him for agreeing to the interview. Ms. Sorrenti already informed them that he turned down other interviews. He is aware, he says, that the artist can ill afford to waste time. They think it will be better to do the interview there instead of waiting for him to get back, because, at poolside, in that gorgeous Caribbean sun a stone's throw from the beach and the palm trees, the photographs will come out much better. From behind the palm trees, a bearded guy is approaching, wearing a khaki safari jacket; a couple of cameras dangle from his neck. He waves with one hand and buttons the last button of his fly with the other.

"This is the photographer. Would you mind sitting here in this lawn chair? Would you mind just wearing your swimming trunks? What made you choose Jamaica for your vacation?

•

". . . Ever since he was a child, he had known he would be an artist. When he was four years old they used to find him drawing in every nook and cranny of the house. In the dark, on any old scrap of paper. He would draw chairs, tables, stacks of dirty dishes, his father, his mother, the maid, and then he would show it all to his sister. At school he would draw (out of the teachers' sight, in the back of his notebooks) medieval battles, or scenes from World War II, or aliens. Once a teacher had caught him sketching a Martian instead of following his math class. When he was fourteen, he had registered at the Escola Massana . . ."

"The municipal art school, in Barcelona."

"He did two years there. Then he took a year off from studying. On Sunday he would go to town squares and to spots around Montjuïc to paint, with a folding easel and a box of oil paints. He worked in a technical studio, as a draughtsman. The following year, when he came back from vacation, he tried to register at the Massana, but he was too late and couldn't get in. He went to the Llotja . . ."

"Another school. Picasso went there as a young man."

"Picasso!"

"He studied there for a year. He painted still lifes, plaster sculptures, live models. He dreamed of having a show. He sent a drawing, which was rejected, to the Ynglada-Guillot competition, and another to the Joan Miró competition, with the same result."

"Those are two drawing awards. You've never heard of them?"

"The following year, he continued studying, but now on his own. He submitted another entry for the Joan Miró award and, this time, he came out forty-second on the list of entries. This had delighted and frustrated him at the same time: so close to an honorable mention, and yet not quite there . . . In desperation, he convinced a friend (whose father had a bar in La Sagrera) . . ."

"A neighborhood in Barcelona."

"He convinced a friend (whose father had a bar in La Sagrera) to talk the man into letting him hang his paintings on the walls of the bar. They did the show, which no one but the habitués of the bar attended (and all they noticed and mentioned to the proprietor of the establishment was that they didn't care for those somewhat stylized paintings of nudes; they preferred the girls on the Damm beer calendars) . . ."

"Damm is a brand name."

"The shows he saw at the gallery of the Architects' Guild, across from the Barcelona cathedral, led him to ponder the issue of the artist in relation to his surroundings at length. He then went through a fervent period of abstraction. Thanks to the articles Alexandre Cirici Pellicer wrote in . . ."

"Alexandre Cirici Pellicer was an art critic. *Serra d'Or* is a monthly magazine, published by the monks at the monastery of Montserrat . . ."

"?"

"No. Not the Caribbean island. The mountain outside Barcelona. . ."

"Thanks to the articles Alexandre Cirici Pellicer wrote in the section on art in *Serra d'Or* he learned about the existence of minimalism, conceptualism, happenings, earth art, arte povera. He went through a radical transformation. He abandoned abstraction, canvas, and acrylic (in his latter abstract period he had finally, not without regrets, switched from oil to acrylic) and, in light of the sheer expense of other media, had opted for photocopies. His first photocopy was of a package of Avecrem Chicken Soup, which he titled *Homage to Andy Warhol.*"

"Avecrem is a brand of instant soup mix . . ."

"Pleased with that experiment, he had done photocopies of a package of Maggi garden vegetable soup, and of a package of Knorr chicken noodle soup, titling them respectively, *Homage to Andy Warhol 2* and *Homage to Andy Warhol 3.* He cut out a strip from *El Capitan Trueno* . . ."

"El Capitan Trueno means 'Captain Thunder'. It was a very popular comic book . . ."

"He cut out a strip from *El Capitan Trueno* and enlarged it on the sly in the photo lab of the advertising firm he worked at (a subsection, as a matter of fact, of the most important printing house in the city, which specialized in labels). Then he stuck a one-*pesseta* stamp with Franco's face on it in a corner, made photocopies of it, and titled it *Homage to Lichtenstein.* Just as he had done on feeling so pleased with the result of the photocopy of the concentrated soup package, he now repeated the operation with a strip from *Roberto Alcázar y Pedrín* and another from *Pequeño Pantera Negra* (likewise enlarged at the photo lab of the studio where he worked)."

"Two more comic books: *Roberto Alcázar y Pedrín* were the names of the characters, like a local Batman and Robin, and the other one means Little Black Panther (no relation to the American Black Panthers) . . ."

"He christened them *Homage to Lichtenstein 2* and *Homage to Lichtenstein 3.* Having done these photocopies with the stamp in one corner, he repeated the *Roberto Alcázar y Pedrín* one but now placing the stamp over Alcázar's face in such a way that this time it appeared to be Franco who was slugging the evildoer. He considered the work original enough not to warrant the 'Homage' epigraph and (after much back and forth between *Good Guys and Bad Guys, Comic Book Heroes,* and even *Comic Book Hero*) he decided on the latter. All that year he devoted himself to producing photocopies following this new plasticity (becoming ever more conscious of the value of art as a political tool), and the next time the Joan Miró award period was announced, he submitted a photocopy of a drawing by Joan Miró, juxtaposed with a photocopy of the 'Help Wanted' section of *La Vanguardia Española."*

"A Barcelona daily, very establishment."

"It did occur to him, though, that if he sent the photocopies *tout court,* they might reject the entry, as it was clearly stipulated that the award was for drawing, so no matter how open they were to modern materials and attitudes, there always had to be a minimum of drawing. Rather than take a chance, he added a few light strokes with Faber Castell pastels and Alpino pencils. For the first time he had had to face the question of the purity of the artist, and for the first time had decided that if a bit of self-corruption (vis-à-vis the aesthetic ideas he was under the sway of at the time) in the use of pencils and pastel meant that his work was to be contemplated by thousands and perhaps even receive an honorable mention (he didn't so much as dream of an award), then a bit of corruption was worth his while. He ended up in eighteenth place, which he considered something of a success, despite the repetition of the frustration of the previous year, not even receiving a mention. Fortunately, he was able to show a series of his photocopies in the Granollers Art Show."

"Granollers is a city close to Barcelona with an outstanding country inn and restaurant: *La Fonda Europa . . .*"

"As a result of his participation in that Art Show, his name appeared (along with those of the other thirty-eight participants) in the review that appeared on the art news page of *Serra d'Or.* He immediately bought a plastic folder with transparent compartments, labeled it PRESS CLIPPINGS, and filed the article away in it, taking great care to make note of the name of the magazine, the number of the issue, and the date on which it had appeared. Right about then he learned about a series of scholarships for art students sponsored by a well-known brand of sparkling wine from the Penedès region. He applied. Doing this had entailed composing a resumé, a primordial step in the life of an artist, the successful completion of which required both a great command of the written word (to shore up weak spots and gloss them over) as well as considerable restraint (so as not to appear self-important). The years proved him to be a master."

"He sent it off, with great anticipation, together with a year-long project to study art in New York. He had vacillated between New York or Paris because, despite his realization that New York had been the center of the art world for decades now, Paris had, shall we way, sentimental appeal for him. As his mother said, 'We Catalans think of Paris as our second home.' In the meantime, he continued working in photocopies and extended his field of interest to photography (non-realistic photography, of course). He had been particularly interested in Polaroids, which obviated the whole bothersome development process, and which seemed to him—in a certain sense, regrettably—to be one-of-a-kind pieces. Unexpectedly, one day they notified him that he had received the grant, and that the official award ceremony would take place at the Barcelona headquarters of the renowned brand of sparkling wine. He was so overcome with joy that he got drunk that night (for the first time in his life) with the friend whose father had a bar in La Sagrera, with whom he still maintained a solid friendship. Not everything was a bed of roses, though: Humbert's mother was disconsolate at her son's imminent parting, which (in conjunction with the recent decision of her daughter, Humbert's only sister, to live with a group of friends in a commune) was the partial cause, it would seem, of her having a nervous breakdown. Despite his attempts to convince her of the benefits for his career of a sojourn in the capital city of contemporary art, the woman would suffer a relapse every time she was reminded that his destination was, of all places, New York! (Her notion of which had been formed by the films of the forties and fifties—which was when she had gone to the movies—and, more recently, by television.) What's more, she couldn't quite get it through her head that he could have preferred New York to Paris, Paris being, as it was, a second home to Catalans. Despite all these obstacles, at the age of twenty-three the young man had landed at an airport which he had had a good deal of trouble discovering how to leave. He had jettisoned his job, his studies, his family, and a girlfriend he had been sharing with a classmate ever since his year at the Llotja."

"Before he knew it, the year was over. He had studied a little, met few people, and mostly spent his time wandering around the city. When his scholarship was about to run out, he thought about his next step. After long sleepless nights weighing the pros and cons, he decided to stay, not only because since his move to New York they had cited him twice on the arts page of the aforementioned *Serra d'Or* without his having done a thing, but also because he knew—and he wrote a letter to this effect to his sister—that if he went back to Barcelona he would miss New York very, *very* much. When the scholarship was down to nothing, he found a job as a dishwasher in a Greenwich Village restaurant. The mental confusion that his collision with American art had produced was so great that, ever since his student visa had expired (and he had joined the ranks of the illegal aliens), he had stopped painting. How could he—a stranger in the metropolis—make a place for himself? And how would he know what one ought to be doing at any given moment? From one year to the next, ideas changed, and one pattern of behavior was exchanged for another . . . One day, up in arms, a painter friend of his (an ex-conceptualist who was currently a hyperrealist) told him about a book he had read on the so-called modern arts by the most prestigious practitioner of New Journalism. Humbert bought it and devoured it. He found it extraordinary. Where his friend had seen only a sterile send-up, Humbert discovered a critique of a variety of errors; where his friend had found 'facile ironies without alternative proposals,' Humbert saw a healthy study of certain excesses, laudable for opening the way for others—perhaps himself?—to correct them. It was apparent to him that if, from the early seventies on, galleries had ceased to sell as they had in the sixties, and if Americans had been basically unimpressed by the whole minimalist thing, the next step was to break away from all that. Confusion notwithstanding, he hadn't shrunk from the task, and only once (after consuming a whole bottle of Kentucky bourbon with a stranger on the Bowery) had he considered abandoning painting and devoting himself to the jazz trumpet."

"Video also fascinated him. He had seen a video camera at the Barcelona Institut de Teatre. Here, though, it was being used in a much freer way. Video's the art of the future, he had declared in a letter to his parents, by way of justifying his third year in New York with his interest in this new medium. Through specialized journals he kept track of the activities of the foremost American video artists. At the end of his third year (now he was making his living as a busboy in a Soho bar), he decided he would just stay and, with the help of a lawyer friend of a friend, he initiated the process of getting permanent residency. At the same time, after all the qualms of those years, he began to paint again and, even more to the point, to paint on canvas. For two years he painted and painted every morning, and on Sundays from sunrise to sunset, before going in to work at the restaurant (the fifth year he had advanced to being a waiter in TriBeCa, which led him to believe that if he continued along this path, working in restaurants farther and farther south in the city, the following year he would be working at the World Trade Center, the year after that he'd sink into the estuary, and the year after that he'd surface in Staten Island . . .). When the Mary Boone boom took off and everyone started talking about New Expressionism (or new wave, or new image, or maximalism . . .), Humbert saw that he had not been mistaken in returning to the canvas. He studied the work of those artists. Schnabel seemed perfectly mediocre to him, a total bluff. And the rest of the pack were just more of the same . . . He feverishly devoured the articles on postmodernism that appeared in the city magazines and newspapers . . . He took notes. He made lists in order to derive needed constants. He knew he had to be patient. He thought: 'It was logical for the canvas to have made a comeback.' Wary of futile optimism, though, he knew that the return to the canvas must be undertaken with prudence, mindful of the advances achieved in other mediums. That was why he had begun to work again with all kinds of materials and diverse techniques, even when they seemed to contradict one another. He used fabric, wood, photographs, videotapes, cassettes. For the first time he tried his hand at sculpture. And once in a while, out of nostalgia, he would do a photocopy. Even though he had been told time and time again that using all those mediums, so different from one another, would seem tasteless and lacking in style, Humbert defended himself from such accusations by declaring that it was precisely that lack of style that constituted his personal style. How agents had loved to reject him! They had criticized him with the same ferocity with which now they were hitting themselves in the head for not having had the insight to see that in that 'garish clutter'—as one gallery owner had dismissed his entire oeuvre—was the key to his style. How blind they had been! Impetuous, unprejudiced, pragmatic, and with a keen nose for the new, Humbert

Herrera had sensed that an artistic moment in which—among many other trends—Jack Goldstein of the Metro Pictures gallery could get away with barefaced plagiarism, and take pride in it, was not only an interesting moment artistically, but also one in which things could happen. In Italy, Francesco Clemente, Enzo Cucchi, and Sandro Chia were emerging. In Germany, Rainer Fetting, Anselm Kiefer, Helmut Middendorf . . ."

•

What Humbert did not tell the reporter was that when Heribert Julià had burst onto the scene a few months later, establishing himself as the new star, breaking with and going beyond all those trends without belonging to any of the in-groups, he had decided to dig a bit deeper. The fact that Julià was also from Barcelona—though he had remained aloof from the so-called Catalan colony and had been an American citizen for many years—could only work to his advantage. Helena Sorrenti seemed to hold the key to the situation. Not only did she run the gallery that had launched Julià and established his dominance, she also seemed to be his wife. At the restaurant where he worked, Humbert asked to work only the lunch shift for a month. He followed her. He studied her habits. Sometimes she had dinner at The Odeon. Sometimes at Les Pléiades or Ballato. Once in a great while at Da Silvano. Every Tuesday, though, she had dinner alone in a plain old Blarney Stone, always the same one. That bit of simplicity touched Humbert to the core!

On the fourth Tuesday, he made up his mind. That morning he withdrew all his savings—a pittance—from the bank. At noon he swept his studio, dusted, put fresh sheets on the bed, and lined all his paintings up against the walls. That afternoon he showered, shaved, put on a clean shirt, a jacket, and tennis shoes. That evening, as he walked toward the Blarney Stone, he couldn't stop thinking that maybe that night he wouldn't be going home alone. Outside the restaurant, he stopped for a moment to work up his courage: he opened the door, crossed the room with determination, and sat down at the table where Helena Sorrenti was sitting, all by herself. He introduced himself, still not entirely sure she wouldn't call the waiters over to send him packing, a possibility she did indeed entertain for a few seconds.

H e looks at his feet and finds them to his liking. He wiggles his toes a little. Satisfied with the effect, he picks up a little notebook (which he always carried with him to jot down ideas he will later copy over into the big notebooks) and writes: "My feet. Self-portrait."

Helena was doing laps.

"I don't know why we've bothered to come here when we haven't been to the beach once."

To the beach . . . But what if, suddenly, all the muses descended upon him and he is so far away from the studio that by the time he gets back they've all fled? The mere thought of such a possibility sets his nerves on edge. What if his greatest insights slipped away because he didn't write them down fast enough? Or, even worse, if he is too slow to realize that the fleeting image in his brain is a stroke of genius? How many ideas must fail to materialize, hidden behind layers of veils, not quite able to penetrate his consciousness? What if everything he was able to portray was nothing more than the shadow of the residue of the great ideas that had died in his unconscious? Perhaps he should consult a psychoanalyst who would help him reach the inner world that was lost to him. What about the seconds in which he wasn't thinking? Aren't they, in effect, wasted seconds? Perhaps it is precisely during those seconds that the perfect notion, the greatest he could ever produce, may emerge? And all that thinking, about ideas and images . . . Why think? Each second lost in thought is irretrievable. If, instead of lying there, he were face-to-face with a canvas, he wouldn't have to rationalize at all: the only thing he would have to do would be to allow the image in his brain to secrete its fluid down his arm which, by means of the hand, would transfer it to the canvas, without rationalization, alive, passionately . . .

He leaps to his feet. He goes to the bungalow he's using as a study, next door to the one they are staying in. He drops his sunglasses on the table and finishes a painting he had started the day before, full of people pursuing one another or running around in every direction. He starts a new one: one man strikes another in the stomach and despite the blood that flows from his navel, the victim is laughing.

He finishes the painting, signs it, washes his hands, calls Xano. What a waste of time to have to dial so many numbers. Xano isn't in the hotel. He isn't at the gallery either. Humbert leaves a message. He goes to the pool and has a swim. Helena, who is sunbathing, joins him. Under the whitish-blue water, they play tag. One of those Mexican swimmers, who risk their lives diving into the water from the dizzyingly high cliffs of Acapulco, reaches the pool through a secret tunnel and drags Helena along the ground as she laughs, offering herself to him and resisting him at the same time, arousing him. He wonders: should he get out of the pool and write the idea down, or let the idea run its course. He decides to take a chance. He goes over to Helena and whispers:

"I was imagining you were with one of those Mexican swimmers who dive into the water from the dizzyingly high cliffs of Acapulco . . ."

When they are done, Helena goes off to shower and dress. Humbert stretches out on the grass surrounding the pool. He dreams a dream that's very similar to another he had had recently: it was so simple to fly, you only had to know how to make a certain motion while holding your arms bent, as if they were wings, and move them with the necessary precision.

The sound of the horn of the car that has come to pick them up awakens him. He gets up quickly, showers, and puts on his contact lenses. Every time he does this he remembers those green glasses that had made such an impression in the press at the time of his discovery. Had sticking them on one of the paintings he had done this fall, which would be seen in the Chicago show later this month, been too impulsive?

"Hurry up. They're here to pick us up."

As he put his clothes in two small carry-ons, an idea occurs to him: a woman wearing a raincoat and a skirt is going quickly down a flight of stairs, looking over her shoulder in distress. At the top of the stairs appear the shoes and cuffs of a man's trousers. He takes the small pad from his pocket and makes a note of it.

Back in the bungalow he used as a studio, he sticks the notebooks into another tote bag.

"Tell them to be careful when they move the paintings."

They get into the car. They shut the doors with a sharp click. They take off. Humbert is afraid that the painting of the woman going down the stairs will slip away from him. He should have stayed behind and painted it that same afternoon. Everything had its own precise moment of realization . . .

•

Waiting for their luggage, all the passengers raised the collars of their overcoats and put on their woolen hats. A child is sleeping soundly in the arms of a man in a shirt and tie, with a small carry-on bag, his raincoat folded over his arm. Two Germans are looking at each other and complaining about the cold. A married couple and a twenty-year-old girl are trying their best to speak French to two French girls who don't speak a word of English, even though they are getting in from a month in Toronto. A Santa Claus is picking up his suitcase.

As they go by the enormous cemetery that stretches out on either side of the highway, Humbert thinks he sees a figure draped in white wandering among the tombstones. He makes a note of it in his pocket notebook. He is quite pleased with the previous note he made as they approached the city: "The city, by night, as seen from the air: millions of tiny white, blue, and yellow dots."

Back home, exhausted, they leave their suitcases unopened and get into bed. All at once they are very tired. They fall asleep in each others' arms, and Humbert dreams that he slips from Helena's embrace to go to the house where she had formerly lived with Heribert; this is a duty he has always avoided, though he knows he will have to face it some day. This is the moment, then, and (no longer able to put it off) he is finally on his way. There is something he has to look for (he doesn't quite know what), and he rings the doorbell (not knowing if Heribert still lives there, or if someone else does, or if no one does). When Heribert himself finally opens the door, Humbert asks himself what he would have done if no one had lived there, as he certainly doesn't have the keys. Heribert is a ghostly presence, almost immobile, who smiles at him from the threshold. Humbert is tense; he can't stand Heribert looking at him that way, his mouth in a sarcastic curve, as he had always looked at him since their first meeting. He thinks: "I ought to get rid of him, once and for all." But killing him seemed too awkward, though not half as awkward as he knew it must be in reality. Then he goes out into the inner courtyard of a country house with fig trees in the back, and then into a wheat field, where he runs around amid the tall wheat which is just about ready to be harvested, sticking his head out from time to time to see the bell tower of the town church, gloomy as a blockhouse.

•

"What I'm most interested in (and this is nothing new; what I mean is that it's one of the mainstays of my discourse), what I'm most interested in, as I was saying, is the interrelationship between mediums. What I'd most like to do in this exhibition, you know, where I'm working, above all, in two different mediums (a photographic foundation and paint—and, in this regard, I'd like to stress that it's been interesting for me to get back to oils, even if only to cast the contrast between such diverse techniques in starker relief) is to confront each work with total honesty, stripped of all prior notions, to discover that it is the work itself which has been carrying out its own process. I think this is important. Because what's the point, unless the work itself is taking you where *it* wants to go, what's the point, unless you are nothing more than the . . . the . . . *high priest* of . . . well, the instrument of its creation. A play of opposing shades has taken place (I wouldn't speak of light in this series: I would speak of shades, shades and color), opposed, but reconciled. Shades and textures. Think of the June exhibition, in São Paulo. Oh. That's right, you weren't able to go. Well, so, in that show what I was most interested in, what occupied my space, and my interest, was the background, and the backgrounds. They were the protagonists. Even unfinished, they were the center of my attention. I was interested in their being unfinished. Because even now, in the kind of painting we can say needs no justification, there is an excess of reality. Yes, yes; just think about it. This excess of reality, this *reification of the excess of reality*, holds no interest for me. No interest because it's a step backwards and, at this stage in my artistic discourse, I can't afford to take a step backward. I must go forward, continue forward however I can, because if I stop for a second, bam!, the machinery of the discourse breaks down; and I find myself at an interesting juncture now. You know what? What I'm working on now . . . Well, not working just yet, but considering working on, is iron plates, because what matters most to me is the support of the work: I've worked on paper, on canvas, on wood, on cardboard, on walls, on plastic, on photographic support (for the Chicago show), and now I'm interested in working on metal: on iron, on steel . . . Because I'm interested in the dialectic between one medium and another, between the media. Some time ago (before the trip to Jamaica), I thought of working out a dream sequence, on iron. Just imagine it: dreams, the most ephemeral thing in the world, worked out in such a hard medium . . . This is why I take such an interest in recording my dreams on tape as soon as I wake up, so they won't slip away from me. I'd like to be able to retain them all, written or on tape, filed away. Can you imagine being able to keep a record of all the dreams of your lifetime? It would be like a parallel life. A parallel life that would explain the other life to us. Since we always forget some of them, there's no way to know whether we'd have the key to something if we could remember *absolutely all of them*. Want some jam?"

"No."

"I also get holistic ideas from them, unconscious reflections on the work I'm doing."

"What have you gathered from today's?"

"Nothing, yet."

"It's not good to tell people your dreams. Then everything is out there. I never tell mine to anyone. Just like certain peoples of Africa, who think you are stealing their soul if you photograph them . . ."

"More coffee?"

"Yes."

"But it's easy to tell when what you're saying is revealing more than it appears to; I don't know if I'm being clear . . ."

"No it isn't. I learned that Heribert was going out with another woman precisely because of a dream he told me, and he told it to me without realizing exactly what he was saying. And it's not the first time this has happened to me."

"He was seeing someone else?"

"He was going out with a woman I knew because she was the friend of a friend: Hildegarda, Marino DelNonno's wife. I imagine he went out with other women, too. Before or after her, or before and after her. But I found out about this one from the dream; I think she must have been the one he was most involved with. Mmm. No sugar in the sugar bowl."

"I'll go get you some."

"Not for me, for you. You poured yourself another cup of coffee. I don't take sugar in my coffee, remember?"

"Of course I remember. I don't know what made me think you might want some now. I'm going to get to work."

"Give me a kiss."

•

In the afternoon, Humbert looks over the newspapers. He considers the space they devote to city politics excessive. He reads an article about the alarming spread of herpes, an article on Policarpo Paz García, an article on Fats Waller, an article on unhappiness. He comes across an interesting piece of news: a week before, a man had become a millionaire by playing the lottery. As soon as he collected the money, and before spending a cent on anything else, he went to a casino and bet the lot of it, right down to the last penny. "Surprisingly," the paper says, "he won and multiplied his millions in such a way as to become one of the most notable multimillionaires not only in the city, but in the entire country." Humbert sees a very clear moral to the story: you should never be satisfied with what you have achieved. He also finds the word "surprisingly" out of place: "A thing could happen. If it did happen, that means it could. If it could, then, there was nothing surprising about it."

He also reads a review of the Nina Hagen concert and looks for quite a while at a photo of Cherry Vanilla, who performed at the Ritz. He looks closely at an ad for the Mudd Club. Turning the pages, he comes across the ad for the Metropolitan Opera. Marino DelNonno was singing *Madame Butterfly*. It's been ages since he's been to the opera . . . The music has never meant a thing to him, and he finds the libretti ridiculous, but he loves the sets. He calls to see if there are seats for that evening. There are.

Helena is in the living room, reading a book with illustrations by Folon: into a building that is nothing more than a windowless cube, a stream of men is entering through one door and leaving through the other, going on to enter another, similar building, and once again leave it, and once again enter another . . .

"Would you like to come to the opera?"

"What's got into you?"

"They're doing *Madame Butterfly.*"

"What a bore."

He phones again and reserves one ticket. He puts on his tuxedo. In front of the mirror that takes up an entire wall of the room, end to end, he combs his hair and, unhappy with the results, musses it up again. He puts on a white scarf, picks up his coat, makes sure he has the little notebook in his pocket, gives Helena a kiss on her left cheek, opens the door, closes it, goes out to the garage, takes out the car (a Chevy Malibu, full of dents), and, before going to the theater, stops at the gas station to fill up the tank.

•

The performance leaves him cold. He finds the scenery (the only thing he was really interested in) very unimaginative. He does take a lot of notes, though. He wouldn't mind designing scenery, perhaps not so much for the opera as for classical theater. How can he tell if DelNonno has sung well or poorly? What's it to him if he sang well or poorly? He had almost fallen asleep and had only stayed awake by sketching a view of the stage, the figures of some of the singers, a few profiles of the ladies and gentlemen surrounding him—whose expressions, on seeing him scribble so dutifully, lead him to think they must have taken him for a critic. He remembers it with amusement as he leans on a wall by the door Marino DelNonno will be exiting through.

Finally he comes out, escorting a slim woman with red lips, well-defined eyebrows, and a raincoat that hangs open to reveal an impeccable black tuxedo. She is wearing shoes with stiletto heels, an enormous black bow tie with her white shirt, and she is clinging to DelNonno with joy. They get into the black sedan that is waiting for them. Humbert is already in his own car, following them at a prudent distance. That woman must be Hildegarda. The black sedan drops them off in front of a luxury building in Midtown. Humbert doesn't even consider waiting around. If this is where they live, they might not come out again until the following day, unless they are going to meet up later with friends. But at that time of night, if they are going to meet up with friends somewhere other than their own house, maybe they weren't going home, and this is precisely the house of the friends. Before leaving, he takes down the number of the building and the street.

·

When Helena gets in, Humbert calls out to her from the studio. He has finished up a few canvases that he had left off in the middle weeks ago, and he's painted two more, from the notes he took at the opera. Helena gives him a kiss, looks at the paintings, and asks him what he's doing up at that hour.

"I was so engrossed in the painting that I didn't realize what time it was."

They go to bed, and, even though at first Helena isn't quite sure at the beginning she's in the mood, they have passionate sex. They turn out the light, and four hours later, Humbert has breakfast, gets dressed, picks up the car, drives around, and parks in front of the building DelNonno went into the night before. He buys a sandwich and a newspaper at a deli and eats and reads in the car.

Towards noon, Marino DelNonno leaves the building and stops a cab. Humbert writes in his little notebook: "Series of photos: on someone's trail." He thinks that trying to go up to the DelNonnos' apartment would be fruitless because they live in one of those buildings where the doorman announces the name of each visitor over the internal telephone. He spends an hour and a half trying to come up with a ruse, unsuccessfully. What he does do, though, is fill up the little notebook with notes, and if that doesn't exactly offset his failure to come up with a scheme, it is gratifying, at least.

At 1:15, the woman appears at the door of the building: she is wearing a black raincoat (shiny, very tight in the waist, with a very full skirt), a black hat, great big round earrings, black gloves, black stockings, and black shoes, shiny and high-heeled.

The girl takes a bus; Humbert follows it methodically, trying not to miss her stop. When she gets off of the bus, close to the cathedral, he parks the car in the first space he finds and fills the parking meter with coins.

He watches her walk in front of him. He finds her attractive. He imagines her in Heribert's arms, soft and warm. He gets an erection. He takes out the little notebook. He takes notes as he walks.

He has no doubts about how to approach her. Using the most common, cheesy approach of the neighborhood guys from his teenage years, without more ado he asks her where they've seen each other before.

"Did we meet at . . . ? Were you at the Yacht Club on a motor . . . ? No. Then at that quiche place on . . . ? No, no. Were you at the Paquito D'Rivera concert last week? No, not there. At the opera. That's it. I'm sure. I know you from the opera. You were at the Met last night, weren't you?"

The woman smiles, and in that moment, Humbert is certain he will never know if she did so out of politeness or because the line had amused her.

"Why did you smile just now? Where are you going? What dumb questions, I'm sorry. Am I bothering you? Do you mind if I walk along with you?"

It doesn't matter to him that she doesn't answer. On the sidewalk a silver-painted bald man is imitating the movements of an automaton to such perfection that the group of rubberneckers gathered there gives him an ovation. Humbert would like to be capable of performing in public, doing something like that man is doing. He takes out the little notebook and jots down in the last remaining corner: "Silver-painted man moves like a robot. Reflect upon this. Body art?" He adds another line: "Hildegarda's face, watching him: joyful."

"What are you writing down?"

"I take notes so I won't forget what I have to do."

The woman smiles at him. Humbert thinks it is the prettiest smile anyone has ever smiled at him. He would like to kiss her on the spot. He wants to embrace her, feel the warmth of her body. He wants to kiss her from her toes to her eyelids. He wants to caress her, make love to her (make love to her?) without even undressing her. He would have gone to the ends of the earth with her, traversing deserts and streams, glacial crevasses . . . Note in notebook: "Review (and, if necessary, recover) romantic symbolism." He takes her hand and kisses it.

"Are you crazy, what are you doing?"

•

"Are you crazy, what are you doing? We don't even know each others' names."

She laughs with her white teeth, gossamer lips, and brilliant eyes, dark as the night. He feels he has never met a woman like her. They kiss and caress each other. Humbert has successfully undone her bra without taking off her sweater. They are in the car, close to the docks and meatpacking houses, parked on a silent and deserted street. Humbert isn't entirely sure whether the possibility of some guy's showing up with a knife adds excitement to the moment or not. She takes off her hat. He kisses her again, and her lips open like a shell. He tells her his name is Humbert.

"My name is Alexandra."

Was this some kind of joke . . . ?

"Alexandra?"

"Yes. Don't you like it? You made a face. It's not such a strange name . . ."

"You're kidding."

"What do you mean?"

He knows by the way she looks at him that she isn't kidding. Her name is Alexandra and it has never been Hildegarda, and never will be, and she will never be the Hildegarda he thought he had in his arms. All at once those supple lips, those legs wrapped in black, that tiny skirt that Humbert has slowly been pushing up, make no sense at all . . . He tries to visualize a scene that will keep him from losing interest in the woman, at least sexually. He tries to forget that her name is Alexandra, he tries firmly to believe that this is Hildegarda and that Marino himself, dressed as if he were onstage in *Madame Butterfly*, was offering her, Madame Butterfly herself, to him personally: "Here. Do as you wish with her. See how soft she is. She'll do anything you ask." But it doesn't work. The woman is not Hildegarda, and only with his eyes closed is he able to go on, follow the ritual, undress her partially, allow her to undress him partially, and finish up in a hurry, murmuring trivial excuses, leaving her at her door, taking out the notebook to write down a number he will never use, giving her a fake number, not even waving goodbye when he drives away.

H e looks up the name DelNonno in the telephone book. He calls a few numbers that could be Marino DelNonno's, but aren't. He puts on his tuxedo.

"Since you don't like the opera, I'm not going to ask you if you want to come along," says Humbert, not unaware that, having formulated the offer in this way, Helena might just decide that she would like to come along.

"You're going to the opera again? What's gotten into you?"

"It intrigues me."

"It must. No, I'm not coming. Give me a kiss when you get home. And another one right now."

·

This time Marino DelNonno leaves the theater with a man. They go for martinis at a bar by the opera house that's strung with Christmas lights.

Humbert double-parks in front of the bar and waits. When they finally come out, they say goodbye right at the door. DelNonno stops a cab and gets in. Humbert follows him. The street where the taxi drops DelNonno is not the same one as the night before. The building is small, but similarly sumptuous. He takes down the address in a new little notebook. He calculates the possibilities of spending the night waiting. From a nearby phone booth he calls information in case DelNonno's number is listed, but not yet in the phone book. No new DelNonno. The phone must be listed under his wife's name. What is Hildegarda's last name? If only there were reverse listings, by address . . . After a while he calls information again.

It's a different voice. He requests the phone numbers for that building, claiming not to know the last name of the person under whose name the telephone is listed.

He calls all the numbers, asking to speak with Marino. If the number doesn't correspond to the apartment where DelNonno and Hildegarda live, the response will be unsuspecting. If, as on the previous day, he is at a house that is not his own, Humbert might sense some hesitation on the other end. If nothing comes of it, he can opt either to spend the night or return the following morning, as he did yesterday. From the list of seventeen numbers he had gotten from information, at the ninth he notices a slightly uneasy response. It was a woman's voice; she was not terribly convincing about Marino's not being home.

"Who's calling?"

"Who do you think? Put him on quickly, I have no time to waste. This is urgent."

". . ."

"Do you hear me?"

"But he's not here. Well, let me go make certain."

He doesn't hear the sharp clack receivers make when they are left on a table, or footsteps pattering toward a fictitious inquiry, but rather the silence of a hand over the mouthpiece. Humbert considers the possibility of hanging up. This may not be DelNonno's apartment either, but the home of another girlfriend. But what if it is, in fact, DelNonno's house and that is Hildegarda's voice, trying to screen their calls. They don't leave him time to decide: the other end has gone dead. Humbert smiles. He could have some fun. Blackmail them. Would they be concerned about the press exposing DelNonno's adulteries? He doubts it. These days of libertines and decadents weren't exactly a golden age for blackmailers. He might even be doing him a favor, publicity-wise. Humbert leaves the booth. He is walking toward his car, lost in thought, when the solution opens the door to the building: Marino DelNonno is arranging his scarf and calling for a taxi. The telephone stratagem has produced an effect that perhaps, if it can't exactly be qualified as unexpected, at least is not the one he had initially been after.

He follows the cab, which stops twelve blocks away. DelNonno goes into a new building. Humbert writes down the address. In light of the kind of life this Marino lives, it's possible this is not his house either, but, according to the rules of chance, or intuitively (and right now he doesn't feel like ascertaining which of these lines of thinking makes it clear to him), the probability of DelNonno's living there is almost absolute. He decides to go home.

He opens the door. He finds Helena still wearing her raincoat and boots, looking over some files containing documents from the gallery. He takes them out of her hands, takes her in his arms, kisses her, undresses her.

•

The following morning at nine he has already parked by the corner and is standing in front of the building. He doesn't think either DelNonno or Hildegarda tends to leave the building before nine with any regularity. He goes straight up to the doorman. He intends to ask for Mr. DelNonno, but at the last moment, not quite knowing why, but sensing that it is the right thing to do, he asks for Mrs. DelNonno.

"Whom shall I say is calling?"

He hesitates a second.

"Heribert."

The doorman goes into his booth, unhooks the telephone, and presses a button, the number of which Humbert is unable to see.

"Good morning. Mr. Heribert would like to see Mrs. DelNonno."

When the doorman comes out with a negative response, there's nobody there. Humbert is in a deli, buying sandwiches and beer.

He sits behind the wheel of the car, positioned so as to be able to keep track of everyone who leaves the building. But how is he to know who she is if he has never seen her? Will he have to go after every woman who leaves the building? Recognizing someone he has never seen before is not exactly a task he can leave to mere inspiration.

He realizes he hasn't been taking notes for a while. This whole thing is so entertaining that he can't put his mind to it. It's fascinating to pull on a thread and follow it without knowing if he will find a ball of string or the end of a rope. From the building emerge: a woman dressed in pink, a man dressed in navy blue, a man dressed in gray, a woman dressed in orange, a man dressed in white, a woman dressed in red and black and a woman dressed in beige, a man dressed in pink, a man dressed in yellow, two men dressed in gray, a man dressed in blue and a woman dressed in blue and white, a man dressed in red, a woman dressed in black, and a man dressed in gray and black stripes.

·

At noon, when the sun is at its peak and Humbert has eaten all the sandwiches and drunk all the beers, and is thinking of making another trip to the delicatessen to buy more, Marino leaves the building with a woman. That definitely must be Hildegarda. He follows them with his gaze. They go into the garage next door. Humbert starts the car. When he sees them leave in a black Buick Park Avenue, heading in the opposite direction, he finds himself having to make a U-turn in the middle of the street. The man by the curb with a sandwich cart is forced to pull back in a hurry and backs into a passing ambulance, which doesn't have time to brake and tips him over with a crash.

DelNonno's car stops in front of a glass-and-steel building. Hildegarda gets out. The car takes off, crosses a double line, passes another car, and vanishes down the street.

Humbert gets out of the car and looks at the door of the establishment Hildegarda has gone into. A large neon sign proclaims in stylized letters that this is a Health and Sports Club, that is, a posh gym. The services offered by the club are detailed in a list on the glass door: swimming, tennis, sauna, gymnastics, dance. Dance? He takes out the notebook and makes a note. He never thought of doing anything on dance. He feels good: he hasn't taken any notes in so long that, even though he knows that his lack of fertile ideas is due to his investigation, he was half worrying that his brain was rusting. He pushes the door open.

A very blond girl wearing a t-shirt with the name of the club and a short skirt informs him at length about the facilities the center has to offer. Humbert, who has always shunned all types of physical activity, signs up without even waiting for the girl to finish her promotional spiel.

"Can I start right away?"

"Naturally. We'll be glad to give you a tour of the club."

He has trouble losing his guide. He goes through all the rooms twice, no longer trying to go unnoticed. He goes into the gym, sees people vaulting the horse, flipping on the bars, stretching their arms on the rings. He makes his way through the steam of the sauna. Pretending to be lost, he goes into the women's dressing rooms, eliciting shrieks and giggles. At the pool, he watches as a man dives off the board, twisting his body on its axis like a corkscrew. He wanders through the halls, checking all the tables of the small bar-restaurant on the top floor. He finally finds her in front of a mirror, one of the many women lined up at the wall, lifting one leg delicately behind them and thrusting it forward suddenly, as they double their trunks over . . . When he sees her face up close, the few doubts he is still harboring are immediately erased: this is Hildegarda, it is unquestionably she. This was the face that had filled all the canvases of Heribert Julià's final period like an obsession, until he had started drawing himself, getting more and more lost in a maze of self-portraits and men seen from behind, exhausted and leaning on any surface they could find.

How should he approach her? With self-assurance, he could approach her any old way and make a success of it. But he wants his method to be so perfect that, for the first time, he decides to reflect on it. One by one, he discovers the defects in each of the plans he comes up with. His imagination is prolific, though, and he continually conjures up new ones. He imagines and, applying his fine critical faculties, rejects so many that, before he knows it, she is on her way out. Defenseless, he can't find the wherewithal to follow her and launch right in without further ado. He decides to think about it some more, and more calmly, and puts off any action until the following day.

•

Humbert tells Helena that he roams around the city from one place to another, looking at buildings he has looked at a thousand times and discovering new facets to them. He follows people and watches where they go, how they sit on a bench, how they grab the handle to get onto the bus, how they open the newspaper, how they put their handkerchiefs away after blowing their noses, how they put one foot before the other, time and again, when they walk. Habitual behavior seems more and more strange to him every day, with careful observation.

"And what will come of it all?"

"All what?"

"All this observation?"

Following people will enable him to learn things he will then make use of to advance even farther, to break with what he has created thus far, to take the leap that will put even more distance between him and the crowd, turning meters of separation into kilometers, atop all the tops, an aerostatic balloon soaring over the cupolas of all cathedrals. He realizes that, unthinkingly, he is taking the excuse he invented for Helena for the truth, and even elaborating a theory based on it. He takes out the little notebook and writes: "Tell a lie. Believe it. Elaborate a thought based on the lie, a thought which, brilliant though it might be, is of no use, based as it is on a falsehood." He is about to add one more detail when he realizes that Helena is sound asleep and he turns out the light.

•

Bright and early the next morning Humbert is on his way to the club. He spends the morning doing simple exercises and checking out the dance studio from time to time, to see if Hildegarda is there. In the afternoon he does laps, drinks soft drinks at the bar, reads the newspaper, and fills a few pages of the notebook with notes.

Around 9:00 P.M. he gives up on waiting. He goes home, has coffee and donuts for supper, gets right into bed, and when Helena gets in at 3:30, he turns over and gives her a hug.

In the morning, at the club, he has a sauna and plays tennis with a fat man with glasses who has asked him to play. Not only does he defeat him soundly, but with his final stroke he smashes the ball and leaves the lenses of his opponent's eyeglasses in pieces. Once in a while, he goes to the dance studio, hoping to find her there. In vain. That afternoon, at a table in the bar of the club, he fills up his little notebook with a list of possible sports-related paintings. What if he based his January show on the topic? Would it be enough of a novelty, or was it better to pursue the idea of working out the dream series in iron? He makes a note: "January exhibit based on sports? Include allusions to George Bellows?"

At 8:30, he goes home. He has a chicken sandwich and orange juice for dinner. He goes to bed early. Helena is there, reading an *Art and Artists* from many years before. Scattered about the sheets are issues of *Artforum*, *Arts*, two months of *ArtNews*, one *Arts Magazine*, and the previous week's *Arts Weekly*. For a moment he tries to suss out which articles Helena is interested in, but sleep quickly overcomes him and he falls asleep.

In the morning Humbert lifts weights and, from time to time, stops by the dance studio. Around noon he finally sees her, on the floor, twisted into a knot, spreading her arms and lifting her head. He goes wild with joy, his heart beating like a cuckoo clock.

When Hildegarda gets out of the shower (an hour and a half later, her dance session over for the day), she runs into Humbert (who, meanwhile, had also showered and dressed), who introduces himself straight off. Hildegarda says she has heard of him and, since she, too, is very interested in painting, she's pleased to meet him. Humbert confesses that he has wanted to paint her since the very first time he saw her on the dance studio floor. Hildegarda asks him if he's been going to the club for very long, because she's never seen him before. Humbert says a couple of years, but he doesn't go very often: work and all . . . Humbert thinks of a painting in which Hildegarda appears, languid and pallid, surrounded by trees and plants . . . What an effect that painting would have in January's big show! Forget sports. Now he decides it will revolve around a single person: fifty, sixty, eighty, a hundred paintings of Hildegarda. How mediocre Heribert's paintings of her would seem in comparison with the ones he, inflamed with a consuming passion, would do! He can already see the titles in the art reviews: "Toward a new romanticism?" To escape such labeling, he thinks, he could do each painting in a different style, forgotten or a bit out of vogue, which could be regarded as new: new cubism, new op (or new figurative perceptual abstraction), new Dadaism (Hildegarda dressed as the Mona Lisa with a landscape of factories in the background, with a mustache like the one Duchamp affixed to Leonardo's), new neo-classicism (Hildegarda as a Homeric Helen out of a painting by Poussin), new pop (Hildegarda as Wonder Woman, destroying the face of the bad guy with a single blow, in a three meter by three meter comic strip), new baroque (Caravaggio's Virgin with Hildegarda's face), new romanticism (Hildegarda as one of the women at Delacroix's death of Sardanapalus). Hildegarda says she doesn't know what to say.

"Say yes."

"Yes."

"When can we meet?"

"I'll come to your studio."

"No, not to the studio. I'll do studies of you on the street. I see this as something alive, completely spontaneous . . ."

Hildegarda tells him that another painter had asked her to pose for him, a long time ago.

"But he must not have done anything with the paintings in the end, because I've been waiting for him to do a show, to see if I had been an inspiration to him, but he's never done another exhibition. You don't hear anything about him these days. We were good friends. Maybe you know him . . ."

Humbert looks at her: she is wearing a black wool pullover with a deep V-neckline front and back, a straight gray skirt, big earrings, a wide, shiny leather belt, black gloves, gray stockings with seams, shoes with five-inch heels, with a great big black bag under her arm.

·

"I have to go. How could you start sketching me now? Call me at home tomorrow."

Tomorrow was too late, Humbert thought. They are sitting on a bench in a park, and Humbert is surprised that there are still pigeons around at that time in the afternoon. Over by another bench a pigeon and a squirrel are staring each other down, motionless.

Humbert asks her if she'd like to go to Chicago with him, to a show he's doing there, which he hadn't planned to go to, and wouldn't, he had just decided, unless she came along. Hildegarda keeps laughing, saying over and over that he's crazy. He takes her hand, looking at her lips, which are so dark red it almost hurts. As he moves in to kiss her, she asks him (without backing off so much as an inch) if he doesn't think he's moving a bit fast. Humbert doesn't know whether to continue along the road leading to those lips, or to turn back. He sees her floating in the air, soaring over the buildings.

She agrees to go to Chicago, though. But they won't be able to leave together, she says, since her husband, who is an opera singer, is in the city now, and he will definitely want to take her to the airport to say good-bye, particularly since the following Wednesday he will be starting his European tour. It would be easy for her to find an excuse for going off suddenly to Chicago: so many years of marriage have created a network of tacit ellipses and accepted ploys that amply justified sudden leave-takings. Humbert confesses that he, too, is married. She kisses him hard, not just closing her eyes, but squeezing them shut, with such ardor that Humbert feels weak and aroused at the same time, seeking closer contact, which she does not want. As they walk toward the place where the car is parked, they set the date. She will go by plane, he will go by car. When they say goodbye, besides kissing, they feverishly caress each other's backs.

•

The problem is how to explain this sudden change in plans to Helena, how to justify his repeatedly having refused to go over the past few weeks, only to change his mind so unexpectedly. He pushes open the door to the house, vaguely certain, though, that it won't be all that hard for him to find a way. There is a surprise awaiting him at home: the whole room is full of people he knows, and some he doesn't, drinking, laughing, and talking at the top of their lungs, inaudible under the waves of music. When he isn't able to locate Helena at first glance, he tries to cross the room discreetly, to the corner where the drinks are set up. Along the way, though, he greets four painters with mustaches who are chatting with one another, a couple of critics, an Ethiopian sculptor whose show has just opened, three women he has never met before (two of whom are twins), and two expressionless men, who are leaning against the wall and contemplating the goings-on, seriously, with drinks in their hands. Finally, he finds Helena, behind a ficus, arguing with an illustrator; they've both pierced the same canapé. He gives her (Helena) a kiss and takes her aside. What are they celebrating?

"Xano. He was supposed to be back today with the latest news, live, about the Japan show, but he hasn't gotten in yet."

Humbert struggles, successfully, to avoid being included in a discussion of art deco, rationalism, and the Nazi aesthetic. At one point, trying to catch a rest from the din in one of the bedrooms, he encounters a luxuriant couple. In the kitchen he finds traces of jam in the mustard pot. Someone must have stuck a knife in without cleaning it. He finds a woman's shoe in the freezer. In the hall, having taken out his notebook to jot down a few impressions, he runs into the double giggle of the twins, who carry him off into one the bedrooms, undress him, and subject him to all manner of abuses. On his return to the living room, dressed only in a Japanese kimono (too short and too tight for him), he finds a cardboard rocking horse in the hall, a whiskey bottle among the potted plants, a turbot in the fruit bowl. They were playing the lying game. The person who seems to have proposed the game is a short guy who is so drunk he can only keep his balance by holding on to the curtains. For a while everyone tells lies that give them away, lies that seem like the truth, boring lies, brilliant lies, pointless lies. Then a critic, who was sitting on top of the television set and nudging a peach someone must have stepped on after it had fallen on the floor with his foot, tells him that his work is extraordinary, that the utilization of diverse methods, styles, and media is neither impoverishing, tacky, nor the greatest farce in the history of art, but rather an enrichment; what's more, it wasn't full of contradictions, as some said; on the contrary: it was one of the most solid *oeuvres* of the century, probably the body of work that was destined to link this century with the next, to make that leap for contemporary art which the great creators of other times had made for their own. The people laughed; Humbert, annoyed, gets up from his chair, and slams his fist into the critic's face without missing a beat. Short, and quite astonished, the guy loses his balance and, trying to clutch on to something, encounters the curtains, which he brings down with him in his fall. Then there is a mass of arms trying to keep Humbert and the critic apart, one or two shrieks, the giggling of the twins, Helena telling him that what he has done is deranged, and Humbert alleging that the critic was out for blood, and even a child would have been offended if someone telling a lie had gone on about how good he was. Helena tells him that maybe he should develop a little humility and self-control and get used to tough criticism. Humbert tells her that, by the way, he has decided to go to Chicago the next day.

Humbert is driving down the highway. He has been at the wheel for more than twelve hours, and he has only stopped once. To compensate, he decides that from that point on he will stop at every bar he comes across.

At the first, he orders a scotch. At the second, a bourbon. At the third, a vodka. At the fourth, a gin. At the fifth, a rye. At the sixth, a glass of wine. At the seventh, a tequila. At the eighth, a rum. At the ninth, an anisette. At the tenth, a cognac. At the eleventh, a martini.

At the thirteenth he sees, right next to the jukebox, a woman who starts out by singing the song that's playing on the machine, then dances to it by herself, and, as it ends, dances to it with another one of the women sitting there. At the fourteenth, he sees an American flag placed symmetrically across from an Irish flag on either side of the mirror between the shelves of drinks, centered on the shiny cash register. At the fifteenth, a drunk is so happy to hear that Humbert has ordered his brand of beer that he turns his own bottle around to show him the label and demonstrate that he, too, is drinking that brand. At the sixteenth, he finds a backed-up toilet that has left puddles of piss all over the floor, which is composed of tiny tiles. He has to slosh through it to get to the bowl. At the seventeenth, he finds a bar with no bar, only tables. Indignant, he turns and leaves. At the eighteenth, he finds the waiter asleep at one end of the bar, and when he raises his voice to wake him, the other customers give him a dirty look. At the nineteenth, they don't let him in because they're closing. At the twentieth, he goes over to the pool table and watches as the player rips a hole in the green felt, and everyone, both the player who made the hole, the other players, and the other customers in the bar, stares at him in silence until he leaves. In the twenty-first he finds a little boy at the bar, drinking sarsaparilla, looking into the eyes of a man who must be his father, who is drinking Curaçao. At the twenty-second, he orders giant clams with horse-radish sauce to go with his drink. At the twenty-third, he orders cheese with onions and mustard on wheat bread. At the twenty-fourth, he orders oysters with lemon, but they don't have any: they've run out.

The twenty-fifth is the bar of a roadside hotel. After having a drink at the bar, he orders an abundant supper, followed by coffee and a glass of whiskey. He looks at his watch: 1:15. He decides to spend the night there. He asks if there are any rooms.

A receptionist (dark, tall, with thick lips, a little under twenty years old, who walks in front of him gently swaying her hips) takes him up to his room, showing little surprise at his having no luggage. She takes her tip with a smile and closes the door softly. Humbert urinates, washes his face, and lies on the bed to rest for five minutes. Since it seems clear to him that he isn't drowsy, and is not likely to fall asleep, he goes back down to the bar.

The bartender asks what he'll have. Humbert would like to see the whole length of the bar full of glasses and more glasses of different sizes and shapes. For starters he orders gin and then, in succession, a whole series of different kinds of drinks. A half hour later that stretch of bar looks like a glassware showcase, until a woman comes out of the kitchen and picks up all the empty glasses, leaving him just the one that is half-full of maraschino. Humbert takes out the little notebook and writes: "Still life of different types of glasses and mugs."

Humbert turns his head. A woman with long curly brown hair, dressed in black and staring at the surface of the liquid in her glass, is sitting two stools down. When she also turns her head to look at him, they both smile. Humbert thinks of initiating an approach, but when he feels his eyelids heavy with sleep, he picks up what money is left, puts it in his pocket, and leaves the bar without looking back.

Once in bed he hears a couple arguing in the next room. Humbert positions his ear closer to the wall. The woman is saying (so loud the whole building could probably hear her) that, although he is indeed a good politi-cian, capable perhaps of being the best—by his standards as well as by hers—he would never really be the *best*, because what he was after was to be the *only* one, to be on the tip of everyone's tongue, every member of the human race, forever after, in every remaining moment of history, and that, the woman said, was impossible. There has never been anyone, no matter how important his or her contribution to the course of history, who isn't a stranger to many. Neither popes, nor emperors, nor film stars, nor pop music idols (when pop music was still producing idols) have ever managed to do it, and neither would he. Humbert takes out the little notebook and takes it all down. The woman is running down a list of great celebrities and asking him how many times a year he thinks of each of them. Without waiting for an answer, she herself responds, hardly ever. He tells her to shut up, and his rebuttal is so garbled that Humbert has trouble understanding any of it. She then says not to take it like that, that she loves him, but that loving him hasn't left her so blind as not to see clearly what was happening to him. He seems to be sobbing. Humbert hears how she starts consoling him, in a lower voice, and how they kiss. He hears whispering, brief laughter. He can even imagine how they are touching each other. Humbert is immediately aroused. He hears the woman moan. He hears some obscenities being whispered by the man that intensify the woman's cries. Humbert begins to stroke himself. The bedsprings in the room next door creak obsessively until the woman breaks out in a long cry, almost at the same moment in which Humbert abundantly stains the sheets and, as he dries himself, hears the cavernous groan of the man.

For a while, everything is quiet. Then the whispering starts up again, more placid this time. Humbert has another erection. He should have taken advantage of the chance to strike up an acquaintance with the girl at the bar. Maybe it isn't too late: he could get dressed and go back down. But most likely she will already have left. Not knowing what to do, he frantically dials the desk and orders a double scotch, and when the same receptionist who had taken him up to the room delivers it, he pulls her into his arms and, between giggles and no-no-nos, drags her to the bed, pushes the wet sheet aside, and kisses her passionately.

•

The following morning he spends his breakfast in the hotel bar trying to imagine which of the couples who occupy the other tables had spent the previous night in the room next to his. He closes his eyes, trying to place the voices, without success. He pays for his breakfast and the room and, as he opens the door, sees two of the chambermaids whispering to each other, looking at him, and shrieking with laughter. He stops, takes out the little notebook, and sketches the hotel, with the two maids at the door, one whispering in the other's ear.

He drives without stopping. When he reaches the town where he had arranged to meet up with Hildegarda, he sees two cars totaled by a recent crash.

He doesn't have to look very far: the hotel is a gigantic skyscraper, boring and extravagant, on the only street in town. The receptionist greets him with a smile. He tells him his wife has already arrived, not fifteen minutes before. He tells him the room number. Humbert bounds up the stairs, two by two. He knocks twice on the door. He hears Hildegarda's voice asking him to wait a moment. But the door had opened when he knocked; it must not have been quite shut. Humbert walks around the room, looking at the items of clothing Hildegarda has left scattered on the bed. He runs his hand over all of them, picks one up, and smells it. Hildegarda opens the bathroom door, wrapped in a towel, and takes little steps in his direction, leaving the floor full of wet footsteps. She hugs him gleefully as he scolds her for having left the door open, and he takes off her towel.

·

When they park by the bar, Humbert realizes that the gas tank is almost empty. They have coffee at a small table by the window. It is beginning to snow. The room smells of boiled cabbage. An extraordinarily fat black cat, like a balloon about to burst, saunters between the tables, rubbing up against the legs of the people sitting there. Humbert finds the animal so disgusting that, when it comes near, he gets up from the chair and goes to sit at another table. Hildegarda shoots the cat a ferocious glare. The cat turns tail and goes over to Humbert's new table. Humbert gets up and goes to the other end of the room. The cat is so bloated that he think just touching it will leave his fingers slathered with lard. If he squashes it, he thinks, he will splatter the walls of the place with grease. When the cat comes over to him yet again, Humbert goes back to Hildegarda's table, asks for the check, and pays, fleeing from the animal's slow and constant gait, that trails him wherever he goes. When Hildegarda opens the door to leave, he closes it instantly, fearful it will follow them out.

In the next town, he also parks on what appears to be the main street. They go into a movie house. In the vestibule, the woman who sells popcorn is eating a chocolate-covered cake. In the theater, once their eyes have adjusted to the dark, they realize there is no one else there. They talk about movies. Though Hildegarda hasn't seen many of the ones he mentions, the few she has seen she really likes. Happy to be alone, they allow themselves to speak in a completely normal tone of voice, in a movie house.

When they leave, the woman who sells popcorn is eating a sandwich and drinking orange juice. It is still snowing. He gets back into the car. Humbert announces that they have been running on empty for quite some time and that they should fill up as soon as they see a gas station.

A little ways beyond the town, to the right, Hildegarda sees the lake. They veer off onto a little road and park lakeside. They kiss and embrace, isolated from the outdoors by the coat of snow that is blanketing them.

•

When they try to start the car, it won't start. Hildegarda says they should have filled the tank. Humbert says, "Ah." They have two alternatives: wait for the snowstorm to peter out or try to walk back. They opt for the latter. Humbert considers offering to go to the gas station himself, but he thinks she could also have offered. They pull up the collars of their coats, pull their hats down over their ears, give each other a hug, and start walking.

When they arrive, over an hour later, they are completely soaked. They buy a can of gasoline and ask the person in charge if he knows anyone who can drive them back. He knows someone who lives in the next town over and runs a taxi service. He arrives twenty minutes later. He takes them on a search that seems unending because in that snowstorm all the roads look alike, and at each fork in the road they end up choosing one side practically at random, only, in the end, to have to turn back and try the other. It is hours before they find the car.

Exhausted and aggravated, they go back to the hotel. They go up to their room and get into bed. Humbert turns over to embrace Hildegarda. She says not right now.

Feeling restless, Humbert tries to figure out if he can get any notes out of all that. Finding nothing, he tries to sleep. Hildegarda asks him if he's sleeping. He says no. Then she starts talking non-stop: somehow out of context, he feels; she tells him that years before she had been involved with a stage actor, precisely at the same time she was a member of a mime troupe. And now she has the same feeling she had when she started losing interest in the opera: she feels she isn't going anywhere with her painting. She asks him if he really thinks she isn't any good. Humbert alleges that he hasn't seen her work and thus has no way of judging. Hildegarda says that the same thrill of satisfaction she had once got with mime, and then with the opera, she was now getting (more and more strongly) with jazz. She asks him his opinion as to what instrument she should try. Humbert, acting as if he were thinking it over, wonders how to evade this monologue that doesn't interest him in the slightest. In his little notebook (which he had left on the night table, just in case) he manages to write: "Woman tells boring story that doesn't interest me at all." He continues to listen until he falls asleep and dreams that he is going out with a girl who had been Heribert's girlfriend but isn't Hildegarda. Since Helena is at his house, they go to hers, but when they open the door, they find it full of cockroaches. Humbert then proposes that they go to his house, where there have never been any roaches, and they would find some pretense for Helena. They go there and the house is a hotel, which greatly reduces the danger of their being found out by Helena. They are so certain that no cockroach has ever entered that house that they are taken by surprise when, upon turning on the lights in their room, a roach appears right in the middle of the bed. When he immediately proceeds to crush it, the juice that oozes out is like thick semen, which obliges them to take off the sheet. They lie down without touching. They fall asleep. Humbert, in the dream he is dreaming in the dream, dreams that he is in a car at Hildegarda's side. She is driving, and she announces that something is wrong with the car. In what appears to be the ideal solution for such cases, she has connected the car with wires to a (disgusting, fat, enormous) dead cat. But Hildegarda tells him that they have to massage the cat; otherwise, the contraption doesn't work.

Humbert goes to massage the cat; when he touches it though, its flesh, soft and putrid, disintegrates and falls off. Humbert realizes that this is only natural, because they hadn't boiled it first. In cases like this, you had to boil the cat so the car could keep going. So they boil it, then, as all these people look on. Thousands upon thousands of roaches start to stream out of it. A spider appears and approaches. The spider is laughing. It goes up to the pot, looks in, and rests a leg on the rim. The people bat it away. It goes off, but remains within eyeshot. From there it observes the scene with disdain. Then it comes close again: dozens of hairy legs in motion, that stupid laugh . . . It sticks its head in the pot again, to see the dead cat (which, dead and all, is surreptitiously laughing) boiling and the roaches streaming out. The people bat it away again, and it exits laughing. Then, in the dream, he awakens from the other dream because the weight of the woman's body (who has rolled over on top of him in her sleep) is smothering him. He gets up to have a drink of water, and a red roach comes up out of the drain of the sink.

·

He wakes up because the weight of Hildegarda's body (who has rolled over on top of him in her sleep) is smothering him. He's thirsty. He remembers woolly fragments of his dream: the weight of a body, a man with the face of an arachnid. He gets up, goes into the bathroom, turns on the faucet, lets the water run a little, looks at himself in the mirror, and, in the silence of the night, hears the sound of the stubble when he runs his hand over his chin. When he lowers his head to drink from the faucet, he sees a cockroach hiding behind the bowl of the sink. He tries to kill it, but can't. Using all his might he manages to separate the sink a bit from the wall (fearing that the tiles, or the sink itself, will crack) forcing it to flee down the tiles to the floor. There he crushes it and stands immobile, looking out of the corner of his eye, expecting a vengeful coalition of hotel roaches to appear. What if he gets into bed and one of those repugnant creatures decides to stroll across his pillow and his face? He gets into bed, covers his whole body with the sheets (cotton sheets, still smelling of detergent), so fresh that no cockroach would ever dare come in contact with them, he thinks, to reassure himself.

Three quarters of an hour later, he deduces that this edginess that is keeping him from sleeping must be insomnia, which he has heard so much about, but never suffered from, and which has so often been said to be an ailment favorable to creative fertility. Is he, then, having insomnia for the first time? He's pleased: new experiences always interest him. Perhaps if he becomes an insomniac he'll be able to devote those long hours of silence and the snoring of others to a deep meditation upon the meaning of his work, to the structuring of a theoretical framework. He walks around the room. He's doesn't want to touch anything, because a cockroach might have skittered over it (except for the sheets, and he doesn't know why he's so sure about the sheets). He can only bring himself to drink water from his hands (not from a glass!) if he tries not to think that a roach could also have strolled down the faucet.

Humbert sits down in a chair at a table against the wall, on which he had left the room key and Hildegarda her pocketbook. He runs the index finger of his right had over the edge of the table and checks it for dust. He hears Hildegarda pull the sheet over her, blow a raspberry, and say what may or may not be a word:

"Budalowkey."

Humbert stops looking at his finger, gets up, goes over to the bed, and sits down. Hildegarda is fast asleep, gripping the edge of the sheet with both hands. What was that "budalowkey" about? What could she be dreaming about? He wishes he could penetrate Hildegarda's dreams . . . And not just Hildegarda's, but anyone's, and learn what everyone is dreaming, see the images they saw, contemplate the combustion of ideas that takes place behind each pair of shut eyes. Humbert brings his face down to hers. He whispers:

"Budalowkey."

She doesn't budge. If only he could get inside the dream, be part of it, answer and ask without bringing down the whole structure in which the other person momentarily lives . . . And "budalowkey," what does that mean? Maybe she said "barliqui-barloqui" in Catalan; no, it was very unlikely she would know the word. In English, "budalowkey" could be something like "but a low key" or "but I locked it." But why? What could these phrases mean? And maybe it wasn't so clearly "budalowkey" after all, but more of a "badalecky" or "battle-hockey" or "Bore a locket."

Hildegarda is stirring; she emits throaty sounds, as if she were carrying on a whole conversation inside. That white expanse of sheet wrapped around a flesh-colored burst of shoulder, and the light shade from the night table, an obsessive greenish blue . . . Humbert gets up, takes the little notebook from the night table, opens it, and begins to sketch: the bed, the night table, the wall, the painting of a snow-covered landscape, the drapes, the door . . . Then he draws the same composition, replacing each object with another: the bed is now an enormous pack of cigarettes; the door, a loudspeaker; the painting, a stamp; the night tables, a pair of dice on either side of the pack of cigarettes; the wall is gone; the drapes are a forest in flames . . . He draws the same scene again: the bed is a dark black spot; the door a soft stain that spreads and spreads until it fills up the whole page. In one corner a boy (a boy or a girl?) plays with a pail. A girl, clearly. Humbert recognizes her at once. It's Helena, from one of those photographs in the album she had first shown him a couple of weeks before: Helena as a little girl, playing on the beach; as a young woman in a little dress, with tacky high-heeled shoes, and a hairdo drenched with spray; with friends on a camping trip; or, now older, with that mysterious Henri, the artist—not French, just an American snob—about whom he knows only that they had been engaged, and from whom some time back he had discovered letters, bound with a rubber band, in her stocking drawer . . . Humbert flips through the little notebook and on a blank page begins to write: "A whole series of brides—in the appropriate gowns—without makeup. Another series of brides with too much makeup. Brides with beautiful faces and fake mustaches. A lame bride, with a crutch. Brides against a backdrop of factories. Brides with their skirts lifted, showing their bushes. A bride leading a dog on a leash. A series of paintings of brides in tuxedos with carnations in their lapels. A groom with a limp penis coming out of his fly. A groom with the bride's bouquet in his hand, striking a serious pose. A group of gentlemen in tuxedos trying to catch the bouquet the bride has tossed as it floats in mid-air. A groom in a tuxedo with high heels. A groom smoking a corn cob pipe, making so much smoke it hides his face. Two men smoking pipes and fistfighting, neither of them dropping the pipe (in pure primary colors in which red predominates). A transatlantic steamer navigating in a sea of blood, with merrymaking on deck: colored lights, streamers, an orchestra . . . Modern warships and aircraft carriers full of soldiers dressed as gladiators. Variation: two aircraft carriers, one next to the other, the guys on one of them, dressed as pirates, going after the guys on the other. A stereotypical pirate, drinking scotch from a bottle of Cutty Sark, with the label in clear view. The bar of a bar: a whole slew of men standing there drinking and in the middle, as if it were absolutely normal, two pirates. The bar of a bar: a whole slew of boys drinking cognac right out of the bottle. A ballroom: a couple dancing, him in a skirt and her in running shoes . . ."

Humbert cannot fathom how some critics can demand—in the name of some sacrosanct consistency—that he amputate part of his imagination. Even if he worked constantly, without a moment's interruption for years and years, he would not have enough time to produce all the things boiling in his head, because each idea is a magician's hat from which new ideas pop up in the form of magicians' hats from which new ideas pop up . . . (He adds the bit about the hats to the list.) What about the idea he had been toying with for days now? Making movies. Not video, no: conventional cinema. He has so many stories to tell . . . For this film he himself would write the script, build the buildings (ah, architecture, how often it, too, had tempted him!), and compose the score, as Charlie Chaplin did. Like Charlie Chaplin, he would act in it, too, because who, if not he, would be able to sense the precise gesture, so subtle that words could not convey it, that each moment of the film would require? And what about the symphonies that course through his head? And current dance, how blah it seems in comparison with all the dances he imagines! And novels: if he ever has time to write one (between painting and painting, symphony and symphony, film and film . . .), how he will shame all the other writers! They will be so mortified that they will have to go home and hide and never show their faces again. And theater: he will set up colossal productions with thousands of actors who will overflow with emotion in amphitheaters and sports stadiums (because his productions will draw such crowds that not even the biggest theater will be big enough to contain the multitudes who will clamor to see this new facet of his art). And poetry? If he ever decides to write a poem, it will be exceedingly brief, containing only the essence: the whole of life condensed in a single phrase; a poem after which no one else will ever be able to write another line. But his activity cannot be limited to the arts; the entire world will be his field of action: he will have all of humanity interpret one sole performance: three or four billion beings, each playing a role in a work that will outlive him and will bring happiness to humankind . . . Perhaps, some day, he'll have to consider politics?

•

Sketch upon sketch, he fills up all the sheets in the little notebook. He is distressed to be left with no working materials. He scratches his neck, goes to the bathroom, and pulls out a paper hand towel. He draws a horizontal line on it. He shades in the bottom. He looks at it. It doesn't please him. He crumples it up into a ball, which he throws into the wastebasket. He pulls out a second paper hand towel . . .

An hour later, when he sticks his hand into the dispenser, he finds there are no towels left. He then moves on to the spare roll of toilet paper in the medicine chest, and when he has used that up, he goes on to what little there is left on the roll. He sketches silhouettes of fleeing men on the bathroom tiles; simple geometric forms on the ceiling; a big face with no features on the mirror; arrows on the floor . . . He goes back into the bedroom. He fills the walls with a spectacular desert landscape: three UFOs are about to land and there's a laughing moon in the background. Then, unsatisfied, he scratches it all out. When his felt-tipped pen runs out, he searches through all his pockets: his shirt, his jacket, his raincoat . . . When he doesn't find a single pen, he opens Hildegarda's purse and empties the contents onto the night table. With her eyebrow pencil he draws the shadow of a woman on the bathroom door and, taking no time to look for another surface, on top of that he draws a pyramid and shades in the volume. On top of that he draws the corner of a room and the figure of a girl studying a boring book, crying shiny tears of silver or mercury, whose brilliance he represents with a multitude of tiny rays. On top of all these figures he draws a horse on fire, a skyscraper with oval windows, a shoe without a sole . . . until the door is nothing but a huge black spot, a tangle of doodles, a mess. Halfway through drawing a hat on the lampshade of the table lamp, the eyebrow pencil runs out on him. He finds a lipstick among Hildegarda's things on the night table. He finishes the hat and decorates the windowpanes with a drawing of what can be seen through the window: the night and a mastodontic building. On top of that, he

draws what might be going on in each of the rooms. The lipstick doesn't
last long, though, but he keeps on drawing, now scratching on the glass
with the metal rim of the lipstick case. When he can't get any more use out
of it, he throws it on the floor, puts on his pajamas, and goes out into the
hall, which is long and carpeted in gray, with cream-colored walls and dozens of doors on either side. Humbert is surprised: the whole hall is full of
pairs of shoes lined up outside the door, waiting to be cleaned. At the door
to room 1030, there is a pair of brown men's shoes, with traces of mud. He
bends down, picks them up, and deposits them in front of door 1034. At
the door to 1035, he gathers up a pair of black men's shoes and takes them
to door 1030. At the door to 1022, he finds one pair of women's green high
heels and one pair of men's gray shoes. He takes the men's shoes and puts
them in the wastebasket next to the elevator. He sniffs the women's shoes
and leaves them at door 1028. At the doorway to room 1033, he turns his
head, looks back at the wastebasket, and finds that it doesn't go with the
rest of the décor. He lifts it up and goes down the stairs to the next floor.
At the door to 904, he sees a pair of navy blue women's flats. He picks
them up and leaves the wastebasket in their place. In exchange, he leaves
the shoes at door 909 and, as he does, hears a conversation inside: a man
and a woman talking, but, hard as he listens, he can't make out the words.
The shoes from 910 he leaves at 914 and the shoes from 914 at 920. He
hasn't got many steps farther when he hears a door open. He doesn't dare
turn around until he hears the door close again. Then he turns slowly
and discovers that the shoes he left at 920 have disappeared. But the ones
he left at 914 are in the same place. Is it possible that the people in 920
opened the door and took the shoes in without realizing that they weren't
theirs, not remembering that they hadn't even left any shoes outside the
door? In front of 932, he hears a door open down the hall. He stands still.
He sees a man stick his head out of room 936, look from side to side, and,
on seeing him, quickly close the door. Humbert finds it so strange that he
stands right there, motionless, on the spot. About a minute later, the door
to room 936 opens again, and the same man sticks his head out again;
seeing him still there, he quickly closes it again. Humbert is trying to
decide whether to knock on that door (he doesn't quite know why: perhaps
to have a little chat) or draw a phenomenal fireworks display on it, when he
sees a man come out of the door to room 943, clinging to a woman who is

kissing him all over. He says goodbye to her softly, closes the door, and, out in the hall, looks uncomfortable when he sees Humbert. Even so, he goes on to door 936, knocks, and when (after quite a while) it opens (Humbert can't see who opens it), he goes in. Ten minutes later, Humbert sees how, without making the slightest bit of noise, the man who previously stuck his head out twice appears, silently closes the door, looks at Humbert out of the corner of his eye (and acts as if he weren't there), and knocks on the door to 943. The same woman, who had just taken such effusive leave of the man who had then gone into room 936, opens it.

Humbert feels that he must make note of all that, but he doesn't have paper or pencil handy and, even if he had, he strongly doubted he would know what he ought to write. He feels a little tired. There he is, running up and down instead of lying in bed. He decides to walk up to his floor, but when he reaches the stairwell, he goes down instead of up.

He goes down to the eighth floor, where he crosses paths with a bellboy who greets him with a broad smile. Humbert buttons one of the buttons on his pajama top.

On the seventh floor, Humbert presses the button to the elevator. He goes down to the concourse level. He goes to the bar. He finds it closed. He gets back into the elevator. He goes up to the fourteenth floor. He walks around, listening at the doors, switching the wastebaskets around. On the twelfth floor, he sits down to rest awhile. On the eleventh, he hears moaning and thudding at door 1109, like someone being hit; at door 1118, he hears a player piano; at door 1132, he hears rock and roll.

He goes down to the tenth floor, goes into his room, lies down on the bed, and looks at the desert landscape he had drawn (and then scratched out) on the wall in front of him until 7:45.

Hildegarda wakes up at 7:45. She opens one eye, looking for Humbert, and sees him lying on the bed, staring fixedly at the wall in front of him. She too turns her gaze toward the wall in front of them: seeing it all marked up, she gapes, gets out of bed, and walks all around the room examining the scrawling all over the place.

They have breakfast at the hotel bar, and taking their time, they make their way to the Art Institute. Humbert spends an eternity in front of *Nighthawks*. Hildegarda sleeps through it, her head resting on his shoulder. Then they go to the gallery. The woman in charge (fat, wearing a polka-dot dress and coke bottle glasses) is very pleased he has decided to come in the end. Hildegarda walks around the room looking over the canvases. They are almost all up, except for one that two men are hanging at that very moment. In the painting, two men (one of whose glasses, fluorescent, are stuck on with glue) are hanging a painting of two men who are hanging a painting.

Humbert phones Helena, who seems to be in a relatively good mood; undoubtedly better than the day before, in any case. She notifies him that they have been able to arrange an exhibition in New Zealand and that Xano has finally got in from Japan. There had been problems with his flight, and he had had to change planes in Los Angeles. She asks what he thinks of the preparations for the show there. Humbert says it looks too crowded and, besides, it was harebrained to open a show on such a strange day, right at year's end. Helena says that it's the fault of the people in Chicago, and that when he gets back he'll have to start working on the New York show. Because—in light of the news that a gallery belonging to the competition is about to fold—she's considering the idea of acquiring it—as it's a good buy—and fixing it up so as to have three galleries in the city. So what does he think of having a triple show instead of a double one, if the deal with the third gallery turns out? Does he think he's up to it? Humbert offers her all kinds of assurances. She shouldn't even think twice about it. Not only does he have it all in his head, he's brimming with energy. He wouldn't shrink from filling up fifty galleries at once. Helena insists that he musn't count on work already completed, as they have already placed it in other shows and, in New York, above all, they need something surprising. She asks him not to let her down as Heribert had so recently and, before him, Hans, Herman . . . When is he coming back? Humbert says he will most likely stay another day, maybe two. Helena tells him she has arranged to spend New Year's Eve at Hannah's house. He says he'll do his best to be there, but he wants to take advantage of his stay to visit a few museums and see some people, and in the event all this takes time and he isn't back by New Year's, she shouldn't worry. She tells him she'd like to spend the last night of their first year together, together. He says he would, too. They blow each other kisses and say goodbye.

The woman from the museum takes them to the door and walks them out to the street. She reminds them that the opening is at 5:00 P.M. They get into the car. A driverless taxi is double-parked there, mostly taking up the parking space in front, but also partly blocking Humbert. Humbert maneuvers, but he is just barely unable to get out. People who double-park, with absolutely no consideration for others, drive him nuts. He steps gently on the gas until he touches the taxi's chassis, and then he floors the accelerator, pushes the taxi forward, and steers it until it bumps into the car in front. Without missing a beat, he maneuvers again and gets out with no difficulty.

They have lunch in a Polish restaurant. They stroke each other's hands across the table. At the table beside them two boys with Asian features discuss baseball. He turns back and contemplates Hildegarda. He centers his attention on her lips, the mere sight of which is enough to bring on an erection.

"Do you like baseball?"

Hildegarda opens her eyes wide (but Humbert hardly notices) and her lips (to say something), but then she stops and smiles. Humbert thinks perhaps he has asked the wrong question, but he's not sure why. Changing tack, he says:

"Do you like sports?"

"..."

"Do you like to swim? I do, I love to swim. Do you like to go jogging? Mountain climbing? When I was young, hiking was one of the sports I liked best. Running, too . . . How about hockey? Many of my relatives have been field hockey players. My grandfather founded a club. Just to be contrary, I played ice hockey in high school . . ."

Hildegarda is watching him.

"What about laughing? I really like to laugh. Do you? I like laughing better than talking. Do you like to talk? Do you like cars? What about cigarettes, what brand do you like best? I prefer unfiltered cigarettes to filtered. What do you like better, vodka or tequila? Between beer and wine, which do you like better? Do you like Italian or German food better? I like both. And what kind of movies do you like better: French or Scandinavian? Do you like French movies better, or American detective novels? When you were little, were you happier during Christmas vacation or summer vacation?"

Humbert looks at Hildegarda with a mixture of tenderness and embarrassment, and squeezes the hand under his affectionately.

"What a lot of nonsense, huh? What time is it?"

Before Hildegarda can look at her watch, though, he has already looked at his own.

"Do you like this watch? It's a Cartier. Do you like men's or women's watches better? Do you like to wear jewelry? What do you think is more flattering on a woman: earrings, necklaces, or bracelets? Do you like earrings on men? And do you prefer they wear one earring or two?"

He stops talking. Just to have something to say, Hildegarda says:

"God, so many questions . . ."

"Ask some, ask some yourself, quickly, the first thing that comes to mind: do you wear your shoes backwards? Have you ever eaten Tibetan food? What's the capital of Liberia? What year was Queen Christina of Sweden born? What's the formula of silver nitrate? What year did Garibaldi die? How many questions in a row are *too many questions in a row*? Why are you holding my hand? Why have you suddenly let it go? Why have you taken it again? Why are you squeezing it tighter now? Do you love me? Do you think I love you? Will we grow old together, you and I? Why does this table have a pink tablecloth, and not white or blue? Why aren't you asking any questions?"

"Because you ask enough for both of us. Shall we get started for the gallery?"

"Not yet. It's early. Would you like to have dinner in an exotic place?"

". . ."

"It's a *real* question. Where do you want to go for dinner?"

"We just had lunch. We haven't even gotten up from the table. Don't even talk to me about dinner."

"No, no, no: where would you like to go for dinner? Surrounded by palm trees, in a solemn building, next to a lake . . . ?"

"We can think about it later, with a restaurant guide in front of us."

"I don't mean what restaurant would you like to have dinner at, I mean what city, what country would you like to have dinner in?"

Hildegarda delicately scratches the nape of her neck.

·

At the airport they find the fewest customers at the Aeromexico desk. They ask what's available. A thin, dark man with blond hair explains the various options. They choose the one that—aside from being the earliest flight and one that doesn't require a visa—seems most logical, since they are at the Aeromexico desk: Mexico City. Hildegarda spends the quarter of an hour licking a chocolate ice cream cone, and Humbert has an orange juice.

A few hours later they are on the Avenida de los Insurgentes, dining in a restaurant, stroking each other's hands under the table, eating out of each other's plates, laughing as they hail a taxi and ask the driver to take them to the airport.

They doze off in a Líneas Aéreas Paraguayas 747. When they reach Asunción, Humbert yawns his way through customs. Hildegarda laughs throughout the bus ride into the city. Humbert is not so sleepy as not to suspect, though, that it may be a little strange (but what exactly does "strange" mean?) to be having a meal of chicken and whiskey, a bottle of beer, and coffee for breakfast, at that time of the day, at a restaurant with blue- and pink-checked tablecloths, only to go dashing back to the airport where they catch an almost-empty plane. Humbert sleeps the whole way, clinging to Hildegarda's arm. She is also sleeping when they reach Tenerife, wondering whether it is fun or not to be having lunch at that time of day, above all not even noticing what they're eating, without time even to take a walk to digest the meal, before finding themselves on another plane that is taking them to Munich where—without even eating—they take another plane to Karachi, where it is already late at night, to have dinner at dawn, and then catch another plane, and have breakfast in Hong Kong in mid-afternoon. At the airport, since the plane they are waiting to board is delayed, they play hopscotch until they hear the announcement of their flight to Wellington, where they have lunch at midnight sharp, hurrying through dessert because—Humbert having no desire to see the country he has taken such pains to exhibit in—the plane that is to take them to Samoa is leaving right away, and they have to take it to get to Pago Pago to have dinner at high noon, speculating in the car that takes them back to the airport as to whether it is acceptable to qualify uncommon behavior as illogical. Once aboard the plane, Humbert reasons that, in point of fact, it was completely acceptable (and therefore possible; that is: normal!) to have lunch in the dark of night and breakfast as the sun goes down, which last they do, in fact, at the Honolulu airport, as they feel too tired to go into the city. They catch the first flight out and land in San Francisco, where they eat three meals in a row, in three contiguous restaurants on Market Street. In the evening they set down in New York on a TWA airplane.

They catch a cab. Humbert thinks he'll have to have his car shipped from the Chicago airport. Hiledgarda sees a great deal of frolicking in the street. She asks the driver what day it is. The driver looks at them in the rearview mirror as if they were drunks who were trying to be funny. But, finally, he says New Year's Eve. Hildegarda suggests they go to Tiziana's house, where there was going to be a party.

When they arrive, midnight has long since passed. For them, though, Tiziana sets the clock back and everyone toasts again, and at each stroke of the clock, they all eat a grape. Humbert puts all the grapes in his mouth at once and chews them, forming a mass of skins that he delicately spits into a planter. A really young guy (who can't quite carry off the perverse role he is affecting) tells him that he likes the exotic custom of eating grapes on the last twelve strokes of the old year. Humbert's champagne glass is empty, and for a moment, he isn't sure it if had been full a short time before, or if it was already empty when they handed it to him, which seems more than improbable. He goes up to a girl (wearing a magician's hat covered in cardboard stars and a golden sun) next to a table (full of objects it takes a while for him to recognize as plates, forks, glasses, hors d'oeuvres, salads, sandwiches, drinks . . .) who has a bottle of champagne in her hand. He hands her his glass, and the girl fills it up and asks him how it's going, if he's having a good time at the party. He doesn't know what to say, so he says yes. He begins to think that he's going to have to come up with a repertoire of topics of conversation. He thinks he'll have to make a list, with all the topics recorded, quite clearly, in a logical order that will ease passage from one to the next without any brusque transitions. A brilliant idea crosses his mind, but he doesn't really feel like taking out his little notebook and writing it down. When he tries to remember it, thirty seconds later, he can't do it: the idea has vanished completely. He lifts the glass of champagne to his lips, sips, swallows the liquid, smiles at the girl, wipes the sweat off his forehead with the back of his hand, dries the back of his hand on his pants, sits down on the windowsill, and hears the sound of a bottle of champagne breaking as someone pours champagne all over him. He thinks of writing down: "Painting divided into two parts: in the first, one man pours champagne over another's suit; in the second, the other gets up and sticks a dagger into the body of the first," but to write all that down seems like such an effort—such a tremendous effort—that he lets the idea slip away. He thinks of writing down "Man from whom ideas get away, or who lets ideas get away from him", but it seems like such a boring idea, so inane . . .

He gets up. He tries to cross the room discreetly, to the corner where the bar is set up. On the way, he greets four painters with mustaches who are chatting with one another, a couple of critics, an Ethiopian sculptor whose show has just opened (why, all of a sudden, are there so many people from the art world at the party?), three women he has never met before (two of whom are twins), and two expressionless men with drinks in their hands, who are leaning against the wall and contemplating the goings-on, seriously, with drinks in their hands. He finds Hildegarda, behind a ficus, arguing with an illustrator; they've both pierced the same canapé. He gives her (Hildegarda) a kiss, with the uncomfortable feeling that he's done this before.

Humbert struggles, successfully, to avoid being included in a discussion of art deco, rationalism, and the Nazi aesthetic. At one point, trying to catch a rest from the din in one of the bedrooms, he encounters a luxuriant couple. In the kitchen he finds traces of jam in the mustard pot. Someone must have stuck a knife in without cleaning it. He finds a woman's shoe in the freezer. In the hall, having taken out his notebook to jot down a few impressions, he runs into the double giggle of the twins, who carry him off into one the bedrooms, undress him, and subject him to all manner of abuses. On his return to the living room, dressed only in a Japanese kimono (too short and too tight for him), he finds a cardboard rocking horse in the hall, a whiskey bottle among the potted plants, a turbot in the fruit bowl. They were playing the lying game. The person who seems to have proposed the game is a short guy who is so drunk he can only keep his balance by holding on to the curtains. For a while everyone tells lies that give them away, lies that seem like the truth, boring lies, brilliant lies, pointless lies. Then a critic, who was sitting on top of the television set and nudging a peach someone must have stepped on after it had fallen on the floor with his foot, tells him that his work is extraordinary, that the utilization of diverse methods, styles, and media is neither impoverishing, tacky, nor the greatest farce in the history of art, but rather an enrichment; what's more, it wasn't full of contradictions, as some said; on the contrary: it was one of the most solid *oeuvres* of the century, probably the body of work that was destined to link this century with the next, to make that leap for contemporary art which the great creators of other times had made for their own. The people laugh; Humbert, annoyed, gets up from his chair, and without thinking twice, he slams his fist into the critic's face. Short, and quite astonished, the guy loses his balance and, trying to grab on to something, encounters the curtains, which he brings down with him in his fall. Then there is a mass of arms trying to keep Humbert and the critic apart, one or two shrieks, the giggling of the twins, and Hildegarda telling him to calm down. Humbert sits down on the windowsill he had been sitting on a long time before (he feels as if hours have gone by), before getting up to try and discreetly cross the room over to the corner where the drinks are. He closes his eyes and decides to count to a thousand. When he has reached about eight hundred, he notices that someone is spilling champagne on him and immediately begging his pardon. He keeps his eyes closed and goes on counting. He overshoots, though, and reaches 1001. When he opens his eyes, he sees Hildegarda drying off the champagne spot on his shirt with a paper towel. He does the same thing: he grabs the paper towel and dries an imaginary spot of champagne on her. She says:

"What are you doing?"

He responds:

"What are you doing?

When she puts her hands on her hips and looks questioningly at him, he puts his hands on his hips and looks questioningly at her. She says to him:

"What are you up to?"

He answers:

"What are you up to?"

She says:

"Are you mimicking me?"

He says:

"Are you mimicking me?"

When she thumbs her nose at him, he thumbs his nose at her. When she slaps her cheek, he slaps his cheek. When she sticks out her tongue at him, he sticks out his tongue at her. When she raises her fist as if she's about to take a swing at him, he raises his fist as if he's about to take a swing at her. When Tiziana asks them what they're doing, Hildegarda points at him and says:

"This nut is mimicking me, like a little kid."

"This nut is mimicking me, like a little kid," says Humbert, pointing at her.

In the early morning, when they leave the party, they give goodbye kisses and say the same parting phrases to every guest, successively. Out in the street, they both stick out their arms to flag a cab. When Hildegarda announces the name of the town they're going to, Heribert repeats it.

When they get there, and Hildegarda gets out of the cab without paying, Humbert does the same. When Hildegarda goes back and pays the driver, Humbert pays him again. They open the door to the street twice (once each). They open two bottles of champagne, each filling the other's glass. When Hildegarda laughs, Humbert laughs. When Hildegarda cries out in fury, Humbert cries out in fury. They get into bed. Hildegarda turns over on her left side and puts her arm under the pillow. Humbert turns over on his left side and puts his arm under the pillow. As soon as he hears her sleeping, he, too, falls asleep, but it's a waking sleep. That is: he sleeps, entirely conscious that he's sleeping, and this so unnerves him that he has a premonition: if on New Year's Eve night he doesn't manage to fall asleep right away (or if, once asleep, he wakes up again), not only will he never sleep peacefully again, but the year that is beginning will be the first in an interminable series of years (which will only end with his death) full of insomnia, night and day, and that, forevermore, even asleep he will dream that he is having insomnia, and this torment will reach such a point that he'll never know if he really is an insomniac or if he is dreaming he is: if it is true that he gets into bed and isn't able to sleep, or if it is all a figment of his imagination (and, if he is really awake, he will be consumed by doubt as to whether that night will turn into another terrible night of insomnia or if, in fact, it is no more than a passing waking state which will disappear a few minutes later when he sinks easily into the cocoon of sleep). Sometimes, the very disquiet of not knowing what will happen to him will keep him even wider awake. It will be useless for him to try to calm himself down, to think that he will soon be dreaming of blue canals, that he will be a boat without a rudder, carried off by shards of light half-erased by fog and dampness, by the lapping of the water against the wood of the dock, because he'll never again know if the dock is the dream or the waking state. As a child he had understood that it was useless to count sheep, that it didn't get you anywhere or help in the slightest, and that, instead of bringing on drowsiness, it ruins it beyond repair. Sometimes he will get up, go out to the kitchen, open the refrigerator, drink a glass of water (observing the slow advance of the cockroaches with horror), urinate, open the window, look out at the street . . . Sometimes, above all at the beginning, he'll pick out a book at random, naively supposing that reading it will help him fall asleep, unaware that a change has taken place in him, far more sweeping than the passage from one year to the next, so that never again will he be able to read things as he had before, nor observe objects with the same casual familiarity as he had until now, and he will find himself having to learn all over again how to walk, to move, to bring the spoon up to his mouth, to talk, to look at each and every one of the objects that surround him, to understand so many things that until now had seemed perfectly comprehensible, and he will even lose interest in what he had, until now, believed to be the unassailable focus of his behavior. At times, he will sit down to relax on the sofa, and it will be there, on that very sofa, that he will awaken the following day, not having rested, so fatigued that he will not even have the wherewithal to lift his hand to pick up the pencil and hone it down to a fine point before sticking it into the throat of a dog, which is a robot, which is a flame, which is a bloated tiger (more like a cat), which is a horse rearing on its hind legs, which is a Hussar in battle, which is a hooker shaking off sleep, which is a sack falling to the ground, which is a gust of wind blowing over the entire planet, which is an orange falling from a tree and crushing a slew of bicycles, a tin clown, a man throwing himself off a skyscraper, a tunnel.

Quim Monzó was born in Barcelona in 1952. He has been awarded the National Award for fiction, the City of Barcelona Award for fiction, the Prudenci Bertrana Award for fiction, the El Temps Award for best novel, the Lletra d'Or Prize for the best book of the year, and the Catalan Writers' Award; he has been awarded *Serra d'Or* magazine's prestigious Critics' Award four times. He has also translated numerous authors into Catalan, including Truman Capote, J. D. Salinger, and Ernest Hemingway.

Mary Ann Newman is the Director of the Catalan Center at New York University, which is an affiliate of the Institut Ramon Llull. She is a translator, editor, and occasional writer on Catalan culture. In addition to Quim Monzó, she has translated Xavier Rubert de Ventós, Joan Maragall, and Narcis Comadira, among others.

Open Letter—the University of Rochester's nonprofit, literary translation press—is one of only a handful of publishing houses dedicated to increasing access to world literature for English readers. Publishing ten titles in translation each year, Open Letter searches for works that are extraordinary and influential, works that we hope will become the classics of tomorrow.

Making world literature available in English is crucial to opening our cultural borders, and its availability plays a vital role in maintaining a healthy and vibrant book culture. Open Letter strives to cultivate an audience for these works by helping readers discover imaginative, stunning works of fiction and by creating a constellation of international writing that is engaging, stimulating, and enduring.

Current and forthcoming titles from Open Letter include works from France, Germany, Iceland, Russia, South Africa, and numerous other countries.

www.openletterbooks.org

Praise for Quim Monzó

"A gifted writer, he draws well on the rich tradition of Spanish surrealism to put a deliberately paranoic sense of menace in the apparently mundane everyday and also to sustain the lyrical, visionary quality of his imagination."

—*New York Times*

"Quim Monzó is today's best known writer in Catalan. He is also, no exaggeration, one the world's great short-story writers. This novel shows all his idiosyncrasy and originality. We have at last gained the opportunity to read (in English) one of the most original writers of our time."

—*Independent* (London)

"To read this novel is to enter a fictional universe created by an author trapped between aversion to and astonishment at the world in which he has found himself. His almost manic humor is underpinned by a frighteningly bleak vision of daily life."

—*Times Literary Supplement* (London)

**Other Books by Quim Monzó
in English Translation**

The Enormity of the Tragedy

Guadalajara

O'Clock